WHERE Angels GO

Dear Friends,

Merry Christmas from Shirley, Goodness, Mercy and me! These three angels are my most requested characters; many readers have said they don't want to let another Christmas pass without an earthly visitation. So here they are, as well-intentioned and quirky as ever.

This year the angels' time is divided between Leavenworth, Washington, my all-time-favorite Christmas town, and Seattle. For the past two years my husband and I have made the trek to Leavenworth the first weekend of December. This town was also featured in *When Christmas Comes,* which was released in 2004 and reprinted in *Home for the Holidays* in 2005. I hope you'll enjoy a return visit, too!

In *Where Angels Go,* one of the characters experiences something that happened to my father. Shortly before he died, Dad believed he saw an angel. Like the character Harry, my father—still living in his own home—got up in the middle of the night but hadn't taken his walker with him. Then he found he was too weak to make it back to bed. That was when his angel appeared. My father described him in great detail: a middle-aged man wearing overalls, like a farmer. He showed up at the end of the hallway and my father said, "Hey, buddy, I could use some help here." The "farmer" assisted him into his bed and then was gone.

Some people might suggest that my father's "visitation" was a result of all the drugs he was on—but, like him, I prefer to believe that it was an angel.

Another character in this story, Beth, plays an online game called World of Warcraft. This is, in fact, a real game and I have to thank my husband for his unstinting efforts in handling the research (not that he was complaining, mind you!). So thank you, Wayne—and you *will* reach level 60 one day.

Merry Christmas to all! I hope you'll enjoy Shirley, Goodness and Mercy's latest visit.

Debbie Macomber

P.S. I love to hear from my readers. You can reach me through my Web site at www.DebbieMacomber.com or at P.O. Box 1458, Port Orchard, WA 98366.

DEBBIE MACOMBER

WHERE Angels GO

MIRA®

ISBN-13: 978-0-7783-2515-4
ISBN-10:   0-7783-2515-6

WHERE ANGELS GO

Printed in U.S.A.

10 9 8 7 6 5 4 3 2 1

For Debbie Sundberg
Who makes my Christmases beautiful

1

The sights and sounds of Christmas were all around him. At home, the scent of evergreen mingled with ginger and spice, and multicolored lights glittered throughout the house. This was Harry Alderwood's favorite time of year. He'd settled in Leavenworth, Washington, more than five decades ago, and he loved the way this town celebrated Christmas. Despite his eighty-six years and failing health, nothing could dampen his love of the season. Even sitting in Dr.

Snellgrove's office, with its spindly artificial Christmas tree, waiting for what he was sure would be bad news, Harry didn't feel depressed. This appointment would probably drain him for the rest of the day, and yet it seemed pointless. He doubted there was anything left for Dr. Snellgrove to do. His heart was giving out; it was as simple as that.

Harry wasn't afraid of death. He often thought about it, especially with so many of his friends dying. He'd seen death, witnessed it countless times on the beaches of Normandy and the battlefields of Europe in World War II. He'd grieved when his own parents and his older brother, Ted, had passed away. He wasn't afraid, though. Maybe he should be, but why worry about the inevitable?

An exhausted young mother sat across the room, keeping her little girl entertained by reading to her. Looking at them, he found it hard to tell who needed the doctor most, mother or child. Both seemed to be suffering from bad colds. Harry was grateful for the distance between them, since his own immune system was so weak.

Harry knew this would almost certainly be his last Christmas, and that saddened him. He'd always been a man of faith, and that faith had grown stronger as he grew older. Which was a natural progression, he supposed. He wondered if the angels celebrated Christmas in heaven; he suspected they did. Harry figured he'd find out soon enough. Meanwhile, he was determined to make his last Christmas on earth as special as he could for Rosalie. Already he was thinking of what he might do to show his wife of sixty-five years how much he loved her. Leaving Rosalie. That was his one regret....

"Harry Alderwood."

He was caught up in his thoughts, and the nurse had to repeat his name before he heard her. She was a young woman named Kelly Shannon—or was it Shannon Kelly?—but he affectionately called her Nurse Ratched. She didn't seem to mind.

"Harry?"

"Coming." He needed a moment to clamber to his feet. Sometimes he forgot that his legs weren't as steady as they used to be. Not long ago, he didn't have

a problem getting out of a chair, but these days he got
so winded just standing, he could barely walk. Growing old wasn't for sissies, that was for sure.

Using his cane for leverage, he slowly pulled himself upright, smiled at the young mother across from
him and carefully placed one foot in front of the other.
More and more, walking even a few yards was a chore.
Still, he waved off Nurse Ratched's offer of assistance.
He took several deep breaths and winked as he walked
past her. She smiled, adjusting the holly brooch she
wore on her crisp white uniform.

He liked her attention to Christmas. And he was
grateful that she didn't rush him. That was the problem with people these days. They all seemed to be in a
hurry, stepping around him, practically pushing him
aside, in an effort to get ahead in the grocery store or
the parking lot. Didn't these folks realize he was moving as fast as he could? A few years ago, he used to be
just like them, trying to get someplace quickly and
then, once he arrived, wondering why he'd been in
such a hurry.

"Your color's good this morning," Nurse Ratched

said as she held open the door of the examining room and waited for Harry to move inside. "You must be feeling better."

Harry never did understand why other people made assumptions about how he felt. No one really wanted the truth. Well, okay…maybe doctors and nurses did. But when it came to friends and acquaintances, he wasn't interested in discussing his health. He accepted the likelihood of illness and the certainty of death, although he didn't want to get there any sooner than necessary.

"Have a chair." Dr. Snellgrove's nurse pointed to the one against the wall.

It took Harry a long time to reach that chair and sit down again.

The nurse, chattering in a friendly manner, checked his blood pressure, which was normal, took his temperature, which was also normal, and then after asking the usual questions, left the room, closing the door behind her.

Five minutes later, Dr. Snellgrove appeared. Harry still found it a bit disconcerting to have such a young doctor; Paul Snellgrove barely looked old enough to shave, let alone make life-and-death decisions. Harry had met a number of young physicians lately, both men and women. That was a good thing, in his opinion—even though their youth reminded Harry of his own age. But these newly minted doctors tended to be idealistic, which he approved of, and they were up on all the latest technology, treatments and medications. The only problem was that they could be a bit unrealistic, seeing death as the enemy when sometimes, at the end of a long life or debilitating illness, it was a friend. Dr. Snellgrove wasn't like that, though. Three or four years ago, he'd bought out Harry's longtime physician's practice. Harry admired the kid.

"What can I do for you?" Dr. Snellgrove asked, sitting on a stool and sliding it over so he was eye to eye with Harry.

Harry rested both hands on his cane, one on top of the other. "I'm having trouble breathing again." This wasn't a new complaint. It'd gotten worse, though. Twice in the past week, he'd woken in the middle of the night, unable to catch his breath. Both times he'd thought he was dying. He hoped to go gentle and easy, in his sleep or something like that, not sitting up in bed gasping for air and frightening poor Rosalie into a panic.

The young doctor asked him a few more questions. Harry already knew the problem. His heart was tired, which might not be medical terminology but seemed pretty accurate, and sometimes it just took a brief pause. The pacemaker was supposed to help and it'd worked fine for the most part…until recently.

"There's not much I can do for you, Mr. Alderwood, much as I hate to admit it," the physician told him. His eyes were serious as they met Harry's.

Harry appreciated that the other man didn't look away and was willing to tell him the truth. He was ready to release his hold on life. Almost ready. There was one thing he still had to accomplish, one arrangement he still had to make, and he needed enough time to do it. "No new pill?" He'd swallowed an entire pharmacy full now. Twenty-six prescriptions at last count—not all at once, of course. Thankfully, due to his years of military service, the government helped pay the cost of those many expensive drugs.

"No, Harry, I'm sorry. No miracle pills this week."

Harry sighed. He hadn't really expected there would be.

"Your heart's failing," Dr. Snellgrove said. "You know that." Then he frowned. "I see you're using the cane instead of the walker."

Harry hated that blasted walker. "It's at the house."

"Harry, it's December." The physician looked exasperated. "The last thing you need is a fracture."

Harry dismissed Snellgrove's concern.

"I'm well aware that I'm dying," he said, leaning toward the other man. "What I'd like is your best guess of how much time I've got."

"Why is it so important to know?" the doctor asked.

"Because of Rosalie," Harry murmured. "She's forgetful and gets confused now and then, and I don't think she'll do well living on her own." Harry worried about his wife constantly. Even their children didn't realize how bad Rosalie's memory had gotten in the last few years.

Paul Snellgrove reached for Harry's chart and glanced at the top page. "You're still in your own home, right?"

Harry nodded. He and Rosalie had raised their two beautiful daughters in that house on Walnut Avenue. Lorraine and Donna now lived and worked in Seattle and had raised their families there. One or the other came home at least once a month, sometimes more often; his sons-in-law were frequent visitors, as well. Kenny, Lorraine's husband, had strung all their Christmas lights last week and brought him and Rosalie a tree. Oh, yes, Harry knew how fortunate he was in his family, how blessed.

And his grandkids... The four grandkids were adults themselves now and making their own way in life. Being around his grandchildren did Harry's heart more good than any of those pills he gulped down every morning.

"I want to move Rosalie into Liberty Orchard, that new assisted-living complex, before I die," he explained. "It's the best solution for her. For everyone."

The physician nodded. "Anything stopping you?"

"You mean other than Rosalie?" Harry joked. "I just need to convince her. That might take some doing, so I have to know how much time you think I've got."

The young physician calmly appraised him.

His daughters agreed their mother would need help sooner or later, but didn't feel the urgency Harry did. They didn't understand that he couldn't leave this life comfortably unless he knew Rosalie would be properly looked after.

"Tell me straight up," Harry insisted. "It shouldn't be that difficult to tell an old man how much time he's got left." He let the challenge hang between them.

The physician rolled the stool back a couple of inches and made a gesture that was more revealing than anything he might have said. "Harry, I'm not God, so I don't know for sure," he murmured, "but I'll be honest if that's what you want."

"I do," he confirmed.

Dr. Snellgrove slowly exhaled. "The truth is, you could go at any time."

The words rattled Harry. That wasn't what he'd expected to hear. He'd assumed he had a couple of months, possibly until spring. Maybe he'd even last until summer. He took a minute to absorb the reality of his situation, then nodded and said, "Okay."

As if he feared he might have said too much, the physician launched into a lengthy explanation of cardiac rhythms and stenosis and congestive heart failure.

Most of his words slid off Harry; instead, the thought of dying reverberated in his head. When would it happen? Would he have time to arrange for Rosalie's care?

"Don't overtax yourself. Use your walker," Dr. Snellgrove was telling him.

"I will," Harry promised.

"Rest as much as you can," the doctor went on. "And, Mr. Alderwood—Harry—you'll have to stop driving. It's increasingly unsafe."

Harry nodded; he'd already accepted that. More arrangements to make...

No problem there. Harry didn't have the energy to do much more than take the simplest outing. Most days were spent in front of the television. He liked those court shows best, and the Weather Channel, too. The older he got, the more important the weather seemed to be.

In Leavenworth this time of year, it was mostly cold and snowy. The stores around town counted on that snow for their tourist business, especially this close to the holidays. The entire month of December was a Christmas extravaganza here. Every weekend, there was a parade featuring an old-fashioned Father Christmas, a chubby Santa and even the Grinch, followed by a tree-lighting ceremony.

"Is there anything else I can do for you?" the doctor asked as Harry rose awkwardly to his feet.

"You got a new heart for me?" Harry managed a grin.

The other man's face saddened. "Sorry."

Harry thrust out his hand. He wanted to convey his thanks for everything the doctor had done and for his honesty. "Merry Christmas, Doc. And in case I don't see you again, Happy New Year."

Snellgrove shook his hand warmly. "All the best, Harry. To you and your wife."

In the waiting area the nurse handed him his coat, which hung on a peg on the wall. He wrapped the scarf Rosalie had knit him twenty-five years ago around his neck. He still wore it every winter. Rosalie was no longer knitting, which was a shame; she'd been an accomplished knitter. Their kids and grandkids had been the recipients of sweaters and mittens and hats, all kinds of beautifully made things.

Time was… He paused and smiled as he placed his hat on his head. Time was… That phrase came to him more and more often these days. He waited a moment, then slipped his arms into the sleeves of his thick wool coat. It felt heavy on his shoulders, heavier than it had when he'd put it on earlier that morning.

He wished Nurse Ratched a courteous "Merry Christmas" and prepared to leave.

Leaning on his cane, he opened the door and steeled himself against the cold before he made the short trek to his car. Like the doctor, his daughters didn't want him driving anymore or going out on his own. They were right. He'd talk to them about selling the car; maybe he'd call them tonight. In the meanwhile, he'd drive very, very carefully.

The skies were dark and overcast, and the cold cut right through him. He climbed into the driver's seat, then started the engine. A blast of cold air hit him as he turned on the defroster. He shivered; it seemed he was always cold. According to the doctor, being cold indicated poor circulation. In other words, Harry's heart was giving out, and this was just another symptom.

With his gloved hands on the steering wheel, he waited for the windshield to defrost.

He could die anytime.

With that, another realization hit him. He had to convince Rosalie to move as soon as possible. But his wife could be a stubborn woman, and Harry knew he was going to need help.

Bowing his head, he closed his eyes. Harry believed more fervently now than ever, although he hadn't been as faithful about attending church and reading his Bible. But when he did go to Sunday services, he walked away with something he could use in his life—

a sense of God's benevolence and a desire to be right-minded and honorable. The Bible was filled with wisdom—and some darn good stories, too. Rosalie generally went to services. The church was only a few blocks away, and every Sunday morning, his wife was there. Their next-door neighbor drove her or one of the girls did, if either happened to be visiting.

Another thing Harry didn't make a regular practice of was prayer. He regretted that because he believed God answered prayers. He didn't want to bother the Almighty with his own paltry concerns. Seeing that God was dealing with the big stuff like global warming and the problems in the Middle East, it didn't make sense to Harry that He'd have time to worry about one old man. An old man afraid of what would happen to his wife after he died... Only Harry didn't know where else to turn.

The inside of the car became his church. With his head bowed and his eyes closed, he whispered, "Okay, Lord, my time's getting short. I want you to know I accept that. I understand you've got much bigger problems on this earth than mine, and better things to do than listen to an old man like me. Nevertheless, I hope you won't mind if I ask for your help.

"It's about Rosalie, Lord. The house is too much for her all by herself. Without me there to look after her, I'm afraid she'll burn the place down because she'll forget to turn off a burner or start a flood because she forgot the bathwater was running. I know you love her even more than I do and that's a comfort. Show me how to convince her to move into that fancy new complex. Let me warn you, though, Lord, my Rosalie can be stubborn. But then, I guess you've noticed that.

"Lord, when I'm gone, you'll have to take care of her for me." He paused and decided he was taking up too much of God's time, so he added, "Amen."

When he glanced up, the cloud cover had broken and sunshine burst upon the snow, making it shimmer with light. Harry watched it for a long moment, feeling good. The problem now rested in God's hands.

2

Harry's prayer rose upward, higher and higher through the snow-laden branches of the evergreens. His petition to God whisked its way past the thick white clouds, carried by the warm winds of his love to the very desk of the Archangel Gabriel. There it landed.

"Harry Alderwood," Gabriel muttered, turning the pages of the massive book that detailed the prayers and lives of the faithful. "Ah, yes, Harry." Gabriel remembered the older man. Harry didn't pray often and seemed to believe he shouldn't bother God with his petty concerns. Little did the old man know how much God liked to talk to His children, how He longed to listen to them.

Having the ear of God and sharing His love for humans, Gabriel felt tenderness for this man who was so close to making the journey from life into death. In many cases when death was imminent, the veil between heaven and earth was especially thin. Harry accepted that he was dying but he clung to life, fearful of leaving behind those he loved—especially his wife, Rosalie.

Harry's days were few, even fewer than the old man realized, and that brought a certain urgency to his prayer. Unfortunately, Christmas was only eight days away, and Gabriel was swamped with requests.

Two prayers had now reached him, almost simultaneously, from the small Washington town of Leavenworth. The second was from Carter Jackson, a small boy who felt he could trust God more than Santa.

Carter's prayer wouldn't be any easier to answer

than Harry Alderwood's. Requests like this got even more complicated at Christmastime. Heaven was busy, busy, busy. There was work to be done, prayers to be answered, angels to be assigned.

Gabriel studied the list of available Prayer Ambassadors and saw that his three favorite angels were indeed free. Shirley, Goodness and Mercy were close to his heart, but there'd been problems with them in the past.

Lots of problems.

Mercy, for example, tended to become too engrossed with the things of earth. Gabriel shook his head in a mixture of amusement and irritation. No matter how short-handed he was, he dared not let those three visit earth again. Giving Mercy the opportunity to be around forklifts and escalators was asking for trouble.

Not once could Gabriel remember assigning her a prayer request without regretting it afterward. Okay, perhaps *regret* was too strong a word. Mercy always managed to straighten everything out at the last second and he had to admit, she did make him laugh. But Mercy with Harry Alderwood...

"Poor Harry," Gabriel whispered.

"Harry," Mercy repeated from behind him.

She had a bad habit of sneaking up on him and Gabriel did his best not to leap back in surprise. Controlling his reaction, he turned to face the Prayer Ambassador. She was the picture of innocence, wide-eyed and hopeful.

"Did I hear you mention Harry Alderwood?" she asked, as her wings made small rustling sounds. This happened whenever she was excited. The mere prospect of returning to earth had Mercy nearly breathless with anticipation.

"You did," he said.

"If there's any way I could be of service," Mercy volunteered, "I'd be *more* than happy to help."

"I'm sure you would, but there's the small matter of—"

Mercy interrupted him, raising her hand. "If you're going to bring up that unfortunate incident with the aircraft carrier, I want to point out that I've repented."

"Actually," Gabriel said, clearing his throat. "I was thinking about the time you rerouted that 747."

"Oh."

Mercy's cheeks colored, as well they should. That had been the final straw as far as Gabriel was concerned. "I don't know if I can trust you back on earth," he said pensively. But the number of available Prayer Ambassadors was limited....

"Please, please, please, give me another chance," Mercy begged, hands folded.

For all the trouble she caused, Mercy did have a certain knack for getting prayers answered. What humans didn't always grasp was that prayer requests usually required participation on their end. God liked it when His children trusted Him with their needs, but the Almighty Father welcomed human cooperation, too.

"Harry's prayer just arrived," Gabriel said with some hesitation. "He knows his remaining time on earth is brief."

"Doesn't he realize he'll receive a new body once he gets to heaven?" Mercy asked, seeming surprised by the older man's reluctance to leave earth. "It's so much better here."

"He knows," Gabriel said. Perhaps it would be best if he allowed her a view of Harry and Rosalie. "Come and meet Harry," the archangel invited and with one wide sweep of his arm, he whisked away the veil between heaven and earth. A moment later the two of them were able to look down upon the town of Leavenworth.

"Harry, is that you?" Rosalie called when he stepped into the house and closed the door against the bitter December wind.

"It's me," Harry replied in a strained voice. He felt short of breath, and his mind was full of what Dr. Snellgrove had told him. He knew Rosalie couldn't cope without him; he also knew he'd have to trust that God would answer his prayer.

"I have lunch ready," his wife said as he entered the kitchen.

He had little appetite, but Harry couldn't disappoint Rosalie, since she'd made the effort of preparing their meal. At this stage, she only remembered a few of her favorite recipes. Almost always, they had canned soup for dinner. No doubt that was what she'd made for lunch, too.

Food didn't interest Harry much anymore. He ate because it was necessary but without any real enjoyment.

Coming into the kitchen, he saw that he'd guessed correctly. Rosalie had heated up soup. Two steaming bowls filled with bright-red tomato soup sat on the kitchen table. What was left in the small saucepan was boiling madly on the stove. When Rosalie turned her back to bring the silverware to the table, Harry reached over and switched off the burner.

Soon he joined his wife at the round oak table in the small alcove. They bowed their heads, and Harry murmured grace. When he finished, Rosalie smiled softly, her eyes brimming with love. "How did everything go at the doctor's, sweetheart?"

Rather than worry her, Harry simply nodded. "I'm as fit as can be expected for a man of my age."

Rosalie looked back at him with concern. She seemed about to ask him more but changed her mind. He'd told her what she wanted to hear.

"Is soup all right?" she asked.

"It's perfect." Not sure how to broach the subject of moving, Harry swallowed three spoonfuls of his lunch, then paused. This wouldn't be the first time he'd brought it up—far from it. He carefully set his spoon on the place mat.

"How's that nice Dr. Snellgrove?" Rosalie asked, shakily lifting a spoonful of soup to her mouth. She helped herself to crackers from the box and crumbled them in her bowl, one cracker at a time.

"I like him."

"I do, too. Did he give you another prescription?"

Harry shook his head. As it was, the visiting nurse, who stopped by the house every second day, had to use a chart to keep his medications straight.

"You're going to be fine, aren't you?" his wife asked.

Harry saw that her face had tightened with fear. "Of course I am. It's...it's just a matter of getting the proper rest."

She instantly relaxed. "Good. I don't know what I'd do without you."

Harry didn't, either. He sighed. Perhaps he should

take this opportunity to introduce the subject—again. "I was thinking that the upkeep on the house is too much for me." Harry felt that if he described the idea of moving to assisted living as something *he* needed, he might have a better chance of convincing her.

Rosalie ignored the comment. Although her face had wrinkled with age, Harry saw her as he had that first time, sixty-six years ago. She'd worked at the lunch counter at a Woolworth's store in Seattle. Harry had gone over from Yakima to take a short training course, shortly after he'd gotten an underwriting position with the insurance company. He'd worked for the same company for more than forty years.

It had been his first trip to the big city, and the crowds and noise had overwhelmed him. A friend had suggested they stop at the lunch counter for a bite to eat. One look at Rosalie, and he was completely smitten. Until then, he would've scoffed at the very thought of love at first sight. He never did again. One look and he'd fallen head over heels for his beautiful Rosalie.

"Harry?"

He blinked, surprised at the way he'd become immersed in his memories.

"You're finished your lunch?" she asked.

"Yes," he murmured. "I'm not very hungry." She didn't seem to be eating much herself, he noticed.

"I'll fix you something later," Rosalie suggested.

"That would be good." He lingered at the table. "Dr. Snellgrove wants me to use my walker."

Rosalie pinched her lips together. "Haven't I been saying the same thing? If you fall down again, I won't be able to help you up, sweetheart."

This was a problem. A week ago, he'd fallen and, struggle as he might, he couldn't get back on his feet. Rosalie had tried to help and soon they were both exhausted. As a last resort, she'd phoned the fire station. They'd sent out an entire crew, embarrassing Harry no end, although the firefighters couldn't have been nicer. He purposely hadn't mentioned the incident to Dr. Snellgrove. No reason to. He was fine, a bit chagrined, but no worse for wear.

With careful movements, Harry shuffled into the family room and settled down in front of the television. Rosalie carried their soup bowls to the sink and after rinsing them out, sat in her own chair, beside his.

"*Oprah* will be on soon," she informed him.

This was her way of letting him know she'd be watching the talk show. Rosie liked Oprah and Dr. Phil, and while she'd grown forgetful in some areas, she had no trouble remembering when her favorite shows were on. Harry hated to admit it, but he'd come to enjoy them, too. The complete lack of common sense exhibited by some of the folks on those programs continued to astonish him, and he was always heartened by the occasional portrayals of heroism.

"We might think about visiting Liberty Orchard one of these days," he said, reclining in his chair. He reached for the afghan Rosalie had knit him years earlier and spread it on his lap. The cold never seemed to leave him.

"I don't see any rush, do you?" Rosalie asked.

Rather than go into what Dr. Snellgrove had told him, Harry said, "Like I was saying earlier, this house is too much for me now. I don't see any reason to delay. We could put our name in, anyway."

"We can, I suppose," Rosalie reluctantly agreed. "But I'd rather wait until summer."

He didn't want to alarm her and decided to put the discussion off until later. Perhaps after he'd rested...

Gabriel studied Mercy. Her deep-blue eyes brimmed with compassion as she turned to him. "He's very weak."

Gabriel nodded.

"How much longer does he have?" she asked, watching the tender look Rosalie sent her husband as she left her own recliner and walked over to where Harry slept. Rosalie gently tucked the hand-knit blanket around Harry's shoulders and pressed her lips against his brow.

"Not long," Gabriel responded.

"Surely God won't take him until after Christmas?"

"Unfortunately, Harry will leave earth before then."

"Oh, dear. So his prayer request is urgent. Someone has to convince Rosalie to move, and quickly."

"Yes."

"But Christmas is only about a week away!"

No one needed to tell Gabriel that. "I know."

"Oh, my."

"Are you still interested in taking on this request?" he asked, certain she'd change her mind.

Mercy bit her lip, mulling over the situation. This was the most difficult request he'd ever proposed.

"There can be no shenanigans this time," he warned.

"None," she said solemnly. Her gaze remained on the old couple, and the warmth and love that flowed between them.

"Do you think you can help Harry?" Gabriel asked, still unsure. Mercy was so easily distracted....

"I can," she said confidently. She turned again to look at him and Gabriel was shocked to see tears in her eyes. Harry Alderwood had touched Mercy's heart. Gabriel couldn't hope for anything more. Mercy would do everything in her power to prepare both Harry and his wife for a life apart, for death.

3

Beth Fischer couldn't wait to get home from her Seattle job as a paralegal for Barney, Blackburn and Buckley, one of the most prestigious law firms in the state.

The minute she walked into her small downtown condo, she logged on to the computer. As soon as she was on the Internet, she hit the key to bring up the computer game that had enthralled her for months. World of Warcraft had quickly become addictive. Six months ago, one of the attorneys at the office had casually mentioned it; he'd laughingly advised his colleagues to stay away from it because of its enticing qualities. Beth should've listened—but on the other hand, she was glad she hadn't.

While the game loaded, she hurriedly made herself a peanut-butter-and-jelly sandwich and carried it into the small office that served as a guest bedroom on rare occasions. Directly off her kitchen, it was a perfect computer room.

She sank into her comfortable office chair, tucked her shoeless feet beneath her and signed on. Her name was Borincana and she was a hunter. Her pet wolf was called Spot, not the most original name, but it had attracted the attention of a priest named Timixie, who had since teamed up with her. Both were Night Elves and together had risen to level forty.

They were unbeatable and unstoppable, a legend in the annals of online computer games—in their own minds, anyway. Both of them were addicted to the game and met every evening to play, sometimes for hours. They didn't need to be online at the same time but often were.

When Lloyd, the attorney, had commented on this game, Beth had been looking for a mindless way to fill her evenings. She needed something to relax her—and distract her from the fact that all her friends were getting married, one by one.

So far, Beth had served as a bridesmaid in ten weddings. *Ten.* Already three of her friends were parents, and another two were pregnant. If she'd enjoyed crafts, she would've learned to knit or crochet. The truth was, Beth couldn't bear the thought of spending her evenings sitting in front of the television, creating little blankets for all those babies, when the likelihood of her marrying and having a child of her own hovered around zero.

Marriage terrified her. Been there, done that—and failed miserably. Fortunately she was smart enough to realize her mistake. Some people were meant to fall in love, marry and produce the requisite two children, preferably a boy and a girl. Her younger sister, Angela, had done so in record time.

For a while, the pressure was off Beth. Recently, however, her mother had taken up the old refrain.

"Meet someone. Try again." Joyce Fischer hadn't been subtle about it, either.

No, thank you, Mom. Beth wasn't interested and that was all there was to it.

The World of Warcraft was the best alternative she'd found to lonely nights—and the best diversion from talk of marriage and babies. She'd been grateful to find something that was so much fun and so involving. The bonus, of course, was Peter, her Internet partner—the priest Timixie. They chatted by instant message every now and then, congratulating each other on their successes. Like her, Peter seemed to make a point of avoiding relationships.

During the game they teamed up and traveled together, roaming the World of Warcraft landscape, and generally made a great couple—in strictly virtual terms, of course. As far as Beth was concerned, her relationship with Peter via the game was as close as she was willing to get to another man.

Just when life in the alternate universe was getting interesting and another battle seemed imminent, Beth's phone rang. Groaning, she glanced at caller ID and saw that it was her mother. She ignored it and after five rings, the machine picked up.

"Marybeth, I know you're there. Are you playing that blasted computer game again? This is important— we need to discuss Christmas. Call me back within the hour, otherwise I'll drive over to your condo and I don't want to have to do that."

Beth cringed at the sound of her name as much as the message. She'd grown up as Marybeth and had always hated it. For some reason, it reminded her of those girls on reruns of *Hee Haw*. Nevertheless, her mother refused to call her anything else. Beth could see she wouldn't be able to ignore the call. With a sigh, she started to log off.

Right away, Peter instant-messaged her. **Where are you going?**

She typed back. **Sorry. My mother phoned about Christmas and I need to be the dutiful daughter.**

Peter's reply came right away. **I hear you. I'm being pressured, too. My parents are after me to get a life.**

Beth read his comment and nearly laughed out loud. **My mother said almost exactly the same thing to me.**

Where do you live?

This was the most personal question he'd ever asked and she hesitated before replying. **Seattle.**

Get out of here! I do, too.

No way! It was hard to believe they'd been playing this game for nearly six months and yet they'd just discovered they lived in the same city. **Gotta go,** she typed quickly. **I'll be back in half an hour.**

See you then, Peter wrote.

Beth put Borincana and Spot, her animal companion, in hiding, where they'd be safe from attack, and reluctantly reached for the phone. Even as she punched the speed-dial button, she knew that the conversation would have little to do with Christmas. Her mother was trying to find out if Beth was seeing anyone.

As if she'd been sitting by the phone waiting for her call, Joyce answered on the first ring.

"No, Mother, I'm not dating." Beth figured she'd get to the point immediately. That way, she could bypass all the coy questions about coworkers.

"What makes you think I'd ask you something like

that?" her mother returned, obviously offended by her directness.

"Because you always do," Beth countered. She loved her parents and envied them their marriage. If her own had gone half as well, she wouldn't be in this predicament. She and John, her college boyfriend, had been young, barely twenty-one, and immature. Everyone had advised them to wait, but they'd been too impatient, too much in love.

Within six months of the wedding, they'd hated each other. Beth couldn't leave fast enough, and John felt the same. He was as eager to escape their disaster of a marriage as she was.

It was supposed to be a painless and amicable divorce. Everything had gone smoothly; she'd filed because John seemed incapable of doing anything without her pestering him. If something needed to be done, she had to take responsibility because John was utterly helpless.

They couldn't afford attorneys, so they'd gone through the legal documents with the assistance of a law student on campus. They had no material goods to speak of. He'd kept the television and she took the bed. Still had it, in fact, but she'd purchased a new mattress a couple of years ago.

What surprised Beth, what had caught her completely unawares, was the unexpected pain caused by the divorce. This wasn't like breaking up with a boyfriend, which was how she'd assumed it would feel. This was failure with a capital *F.*

Following the divorce, she'd gone to see a counselor, who'd described her emotions as grief. At the time she'd scoffed. She was happy to be rid of John and the marriage, she'd said. Nonetheless, she *had* grieved and in some ways still did. It was perhaps the most intense pain she'd ever experienced. It'd left her emotionally depleted. Nine years later, she was unable to put her failed marriage behind her.

Twice during the divorce proceedings she'd hesitated. Twice she'd considered going to John and making one last effort to work it out. The problem wasn't that she'd found him in bed with another woman or that he'd been abusive, physically or mentally. He wasn't an addict or an alcoholic—just completely irresponsible and immature. She'd had enough, and in the end she'd walked away. Her failure to try again was one of the things that still haunted her.

"Marybeth, I was asking you about Christmas," her mother was saying.

"Oh, sorry, I wasn't paying attention."

"I noticed," Joyce said sarcastically. "Your father and I thought that instead of the big fancy dinner we do every year, we'd have a potluck."

A potluck on Christmas Day? Beth didn't like the sound of that, although she understood the reasoning. Her mother spent most of the day in the kitchen and that couldn't be much fun for her. Beth decided she'd do her share without begrudging the time or expense.

"Aren't you going to complain?" her mother asked as if taken aback by her lack of response.

"No. Actually I was thinking I'd bring the turkey and stuffing."

"You?"

"I can cook." Beth thought the question in her mother's voice bordered on insulting.

"Is that so?" Joyce Fischer asked. "When did you last

eat anything that didn't come from a pizza delivery place or the frozen food section at the grocery store?"

Living alone, Beth didn't have much reason to stand over a stove. Not when it was convenient and easy to order takeout or grab something from the deli. Her microwave got far more use than her stove.

"Okay, okay, I'll order a cooked turkey. We *have* to have turkey, Mom. It's tradition."

"I'd like to begin a new tradition," her mother said. "I want to enjoy the day with my grandkids—speaking of which, when can I expect more?"

Beth was amused by the transition from dinner to her absent love life in one easy breath. "Probably never."

"Marybeth!" She seemed horrified at the prospect. "You're a beautiful woman. You need to put your divorce behind you and move on with your life. You know John has, and more power to him."

Mentioning the fact that her ex-husband had remarried was a low blow.

Lisa Carroll, a college friend of Beth's—correction, acquaintance, and an *un*friendly one at that—had gleefully shared the news of John's marriage a couple of summers ago. Beth had taken it hard, although they'd been divorced for seven years by then. John was perfectly free to try his hand at married life a second time. She was happy for him. Thrilled, even.

That was what she'd tried to tell herself, but it didn't explain the depression she'd sunk into afterward. For weeks she was weepy and miserable. In the back of her mind, she'd held out hope that one day John would return to her. It was an utterly outlandish notion, wholly unrealistic.

"I should never have told you John got married again," she said, unable to disguise the pain of her mother's words.

"I'm sorry, dear. But you do need to move on. I was in church this week and I lit a candle for you. I asked God to send someone special into your life and I feel sure He'll answer my prayer."

"You lit a candle on my behalf?"

"I always do when I have a special prayer."

Beth rolled her eyes. "You asked God to send me a husband?" She couldn't believe her mother would do this.

"Don't make it sound like I signed you up for a dating service."

"That's not what I meant."

"Isn't there *anyone* who interests you?" Joyce pleaded.

The desperation in her mother's voice made Beth uncomfortable. "Not really," she murmured.

"Someone at work?"

"No." Beth most emphatically did not want an office romance. She'd seen a couple of those go sour. After the last one, between a legal secretary and one of the partners, the law firm had set a policy against the practice of dating within the office. Which was fine with Beth, since she happened to enjoy her job and had no intention of risking dismissal.

Her gaze drifted toward the computer screen. "Well, there's someone I met recently…."

"There is?" Hope flared instantly.

You'd think Beth had just announced that she'd set her wedding date.

"We met on WoW."

"That ridiculous game?"

"Yes, Mom. I found out he lives in Seattle."

"What's his name?"

"Peter."

"Invite him to Christmas dinner," Joyce said promptly. "I'll do the full meal. Forget the potluck. I'll entice him with my cooking—and I promise to teach you how. You know what they say about the way to a man's heart."

"Mom!"

"I used to be scornful of those old wives' tales, too," her mother continued undaunted, "but so many of them are true. Now, don't worry, I'll downplay the fact that you don't cook. Leave everything to me." Her mother didn't even attempt to hide her delight.

"Mother, no!" Good grief, for all she knew, Peter was married. She didn't dare ask for fear he'd assume she was interested. All right, she *was* interested, but only because her mother had forced her into it.

"You've got one week to ask him."

"Mother!"

"I insist."

Beth closed her eyes and before she could protest

further, Joyce disconnected the line. Sighing, Beth hung up the phone. It was either arrive on Christmas Day with a man or disappoint her mother. She sighed again as she recalled that Joyce had resorted to prayer in order to find her a husband.

Beth loved her sister and she treasured little James and Bella, her nephew and niece, but Angela hadn't done her any favors by marrying the exemplary Brian and then quickly producing two perfect grandchildren.

Trying to forget her woes, she logged back on to the game and was pleased to see that her partner was still online. She joined Peter and soon afterward he sent her a message.

How'd the conversation with your mother go?

Okay. She wished she hadn't mentioned that she'd be talking to her family. She was more concerned with what had happened while she was Away From the Keyboard. **Did I miss anything exciting when I was AFK?**

Yeah. I teamed up with level 41 Dwarf Warrior and defeated the last two Warmongers to complete the Crushridge quest.

Beth sat up straighter. **Wow. Great going.**

You should've been here. I started pounding my chest.

You Tarzan? she joked.

Only if you're Jane, came his reply.

Beth read the line a second time. He almost seemed to be flirting with her. Nah, he was just teasing, which they often did, bantering back and forth and congratulating each other. It would be easy to misread his intentions, and she didn't want to make more of this than warranted.

When she didn't respond to his comment, they returned to the game. Only later, when she'd logged off and headed for the shower, did Beth pause to reconsider.

If Peter *had* been flirting, and that was a huge *if,* perhaps she should make an effort to learn more about him.

Beth turned on the shower. These were the thoughts of a desperate woman, she told herself grimly. Signs of someone who'd sunk to a new low—finding a date for Christmas Day through an online computer game.

4

Gabriel gazed at Joyce Fischer's prayer request, which had appeared in the Book of Prayers a few days earlier. The book rested on his desk, spread open, filling up almost as quickly as he could make assignments. Joyce had prayed countless times that her daughter would finally meet the right man. Gabriel shook his head as he tapped his finger against the page. It would help if Beth was amenable to a new relationship. After her divorce, Joyce Fischer's daughter had completely closed herself off from men; this Peter, however, might be an interesting prospect.

"Gabriel?" He heard the timid voice of Goodness behind him. Gabriel knew the minute he'd assigned Mercy to Harry Alderwood's request, Mercy's usual companions wouldn't be far behind. It would be just like Shirley and Goodness to want a piece of the action, too. Far be it from them to remain in heaven while Mercy got an assignment on earth.

"About Beth?" Goodness pressed.

The Prayer Ambassador regarded him with imploring eyes. Eyes so blue they seemed to glow. Gabriel wasn't surprised to discover that Goodness had been reading over his shoulder. Apparently she was interested in the Beth Fischer assignment.

"What about her?" Gabriel asked, ignoring the plea in her eyes.

"She could use some help, don't you think?"

"All humans have fallen short," Gabriel explained, and while it was true, he took no pleasure in saying so.

"Which is why God assigned us to help."

He couldn't disagree with that.

"What's going on with Beth?" Goodness asked, stepping closer to Gabriel's desk and eyeing the huge Book of Prayers.

The archangel stepped aside so Goodness could read Joyce Fischer's entire request. He pictured Joyce in St. Alphonsus Catholic Church, kneeling by the altar rail and lighting a candle as she bowed her head and prayed for her daughter. Although Joyce had referred to grandchildren, the real desire of her heart was to see Beth happy. Joyce believed that a relationship, a marriage and family, was the way to make that happen for her daughter. Gabriel felt reasonably sure she was right.

"What about Kevin Goodwin?" Goodness asked.

Gabriel was impressed. Clearly Goodness had already done her research on Beth.

"They work together. Kevin is unattached," Goodness continued.

"True," Gabriel murmured. He'd considered Kevin himself, but apparently God had other plans for the young attorney—plans that didn't include a relationship with Beth. Plus, there *was* the small matter of her company's policy on workplace romance, which created a further complication. "Personally, I like Peter," he said.

Goodness gave him an incredulous look. "From that computer game Beth's hooked on? *That* Peter?"

Gabriel nodded.

Goodness thought about it and when she spoke again, she betrayed her reservations. "He's a possibility, I guess."

Gabriel arched one of his heavy white brows. "You guess?" As endearing as Goodness was, he wouldn't accept insubordination from her or any of the other Prayer Ambassadors.

"Don't misunderstand me, I like Peter quite a bit," Goodness added hurriedly, obviously realizing she'd overstepped some invisible line. She should know by now, Gabriel grumbled to himself, that he took Prayer request protocol seriously.

"It's just that I'm afraid the only way they'll ever be able to communicate is as Night Elves," she said after a moment's pause.

This produced a smile. "Yes, well, the computer game's a concern, but a minor one."

"Beth likes Peter—doesn't she?" Goodness asked.

Gabriel had to reflect on that question carefully. "She's comfortable with him. With what she knows of him, anyway," he finally said.

"That's a start," Goodness murmured in an uncertain voice.

"You have a problem with it?" Gabriel asked, genuinely interested in her reply.

"Not a problem…" Goodness hesitated. "I think it's a sad state of affairs that humans are resorting to relationships through the computer. There's no real intimacy—but I could be wrong. I'll admit *that's* happened before."

Gabriel shrugged. "For some, it's simply an easier way to meet people. In fact, a person's character can be revealed in these role-playing games." He nodded sagely, pleased with his up-to-date observation. "The way Beth and Peter are able to work together as partners, for example."

"I suppose," Goodness agreed with evident reluctance. "I still think it's rather sad."

Gabriel studied her. With her current attitude, he had to wonder if Goodness was the right choice for Beth.

"How's she doing now?" Goodness asked.

"Shall we take a look?"

"Please." Goodness sidled closer to the archangel. "You *are* going to send me to earth, aren't you?"

Those same blue eyes gazed at him expectantly. Goodness wasn't his first choice and he feared this request was too difficult for her. Another Prayer Ambassador, one with a little more experience in complicated situations, might serve better. One who wouldn't be as tempted by things of the earth. Unfortunately—like Mercy—Goodness had a somewhat blemished reputation when it came to her prayer assignments. But even knowing that, Gabriel found he couldn't refuse her. "You can join Mercy."

"Oh, thank you," Goodness trilled, clasping her hands together. Her wings fluttered rapidly with excitement, dropping a feather or two. "I won't disappoint you, Gabriel. You have my word."

"I'm counting on that." He meant it, too. This was too

important an assignment for her to bungle; it needed a delicate hand. He caught himself before warning Goodness. No, Gabriel decided, he'd let her unravel the revelations about Beth all on her own. This presented a growth opportunity for Goodness—and for Beth Fischer, too.

"What's she doing now?" Goodness asked, crowding close to Gabriel in her eagerness to see Beth.

"It's lunchtime," Gabriel said. "She's at a small waterfront restaurant with a friend." With one sweep of his arms, Gabriel parted the veil of clouds that obscured the earth below. At first, the view was hazy, but a few seconds later, the air cleared. Then, as though they were gazing through glass, Gabriel and Goodness saw Beth. She and her friend were seated at a table in a busy restaurant. A wreath in the nearby window was decorated with sprigs of holly and red Christmas balls.

Beth's long dark hair was parted in the middle, and she wore a soft pink cashmere sweater with gray wool pants.

"She looks very pretty," Goodness whispered.

Gabriel could only agree.

* * *

"So, what are your plans for Christmas?" Heidi asked as she picked up half of the tuna-salad sandwich they were sharing.

"I'll spend it with my parents," Beth said without any real enthusiasm. Already she was worried. Her mother had suggested—no, insisted—that Beth invite Peter to join them on Christmas Day. It was an unlikely scenario. After six months of impersonal conversation, she had no idea how they were going to make the transition from being WoW partners to friends to…well, dating each other. Sort of. A Christmas Day blind date—with her family, yet. She grimaced.

How could she possibly convince someone she'd never even seen to accompany her to one of the most important holiday functions of the year? She might as well ask for a miracle.

"You've drifted off again."

Beth didn't need to ask what her friend meant. She often grew quiet when something troubled her. "Can I ask you a question?" Beth asked, setting down her sandwich and leaning toward Heidi.

"Sure, anything. You know that."

Beth considered the other woman one of her best friends. She'd been a member of Heidi's wedding party and was godmother to her son, Adam.

"When you first met Sam…" she began. Heidi and Sam had just begun seeing each other when Beth met her; they'd now been married four years.

"When I first met Sam," Heidi repeated. "Did I know I was going to fall in love with him? Is that what you want to ask?"

Beth blinked. That wasn't *exactly* it, but close enough. "Yes."

"The answer is no. In fact, I thought he was a total nerd. I mean, could you imagine *me* married to an accountant? I found him so fussy and detail-oriented, I couldn't picture the two of us together."

It *was* remarkable. Heidi, her fun-loving, easygoing friend attracted to a bean counter. Yet as far as Beth could tell, they were completely happy in their relationship. They were so different; Heidi was slapdash and impulsive and, as she'd said, Sam was the opposite. But where it truly mattered—their feelings about marriage and family, for instance—their values were the same. Recently, with Heidi's encouragement, Sam had joined a couple of his friends in a new business venture. Their firm, specializing in forensic accounting, was doing well.

"It wasn't like that with John and me," Beth murmured. "When we first met, I was sure we were the perfect match." She swallowed hard. She didn't know why she continued to do this—torturing herself with the details of her failed marriage. All it did was remind her that she simply wasn't any good at relationships.

"John was a long time ago."

This was Heidi's gentle way of urging her to stop dragging the past into the present, and she was right. Sitting up straighter, Beth squared her shoulders. "I think I might have met someone."

That immediately sparked Heidi's interest. In the last five years, she'd frequently tried to introduce Beth to available men, mostly colleagues of Sam's. Beth had declined each and every time. "Who did you meet? Where? When?"

"We met online."

Her friend instantly brightened. "You signed up with one of those Internet dating services?" Heidi had suggested this approach months earlier—advice Beth had strongly rejected.

"No, we met… I mean, we haven't *really* met. We're partners in an online computer game."

"That war thing?" Heidi wrinkled her nose in distaste.

Beth nodded. "We teamed up in World of Warcraft last June. But I know next to nothing about him, other than the fact that he lives in Seattle." Even as she explained this, Beth realized it wasn't true. Peter was decisive, a characteristic she admired in a man. He was thoughtful, too. The two of them worked well together in the landscape of the game, anticipating and complementing each other's moves.

"Then find out more," Heidi urged. "Contact him outside the game. Meet him for coffee or something."

Beth shook her head. "I couldn't do that," she said automatically. And yet she had to, didn't she? Unless she was prepared to disappoint her mother for the thousandth time.

"Why couldn't you?" Heidi asked, genuinely per-plexed. "You said you've been partners for…what? Six months. Make up an excuse. Tell him you want to dis-cuss battle strategy and you'd prefer to do it in the real world."

"But…he might think I'm hitting on him."

Heidi smiled. "Well, aren't you?"

Her friend had a point. "Not really," Beth mumbled but it was a weak rejoinder.

"You want him to meet your family, don't you?"

That was a nerve-racking subject. She decided to tell Heidi the whole story, how all of this had started with her mother's phone call. As she spoke, she con-cluded hopelessly that inviting him to Christmas din-ner was impossible. Actually *bringing* him would be worse. Then again…it might work if there was an understanding between them. But she couldn't figure out why Peter would agree to such an arrangement. He had his own family, his own obligations without taking on hers. No, she couldn't ask him.

On second thought, he *might* understand. He'd said his family was after him to get a life. Perhaps they could join forces the way they had in World of War-craft. Combine their efforts.

Still...

"For all I know he could be fifty, living at home and unemployed." There, it was out—Beth's biggest fear. Of course, Peter could be wondering the same thing about her. "Or—" an even bigger fear "—he could be married."

Chewing her sandwich, Heidi didn't respond for a moment. "The only way to find out is to ask," she said reasonably.

"He might think I'm—"

"What? Available? Beth, you *are* available! Okay, so you made a mistake in judgment. It happens, it's too bad, but it isn't the end of the world!"

"Should I tell Peter right off?" she asked uncertainly. "About my divorce?" This was her other worry—how much to say and when. She was afraid that once they did talk, she'd compulsively blurt out her entire relationship history. After two minutes, her prospective Christmas date would flee for the border.

"Don't lie," Heidi advised.

"Should I be evasive?"

"Don't overload him with details in the beginning. That's all I'm saying."

"Right." It seemed ridiculous to be discussing this when Peter hadn't even agreed to meet her yet.

"You do like what you know about him, right?"

Beth considered the question, then nodded. "Yeah."

"That's the important thing," Heidi assured her.

Beth nodded again. All she needed to do now was take that first step.

Goodness sighed as the veil between heaven and earth slowly closed, blocking the angel's view. She turned to Gabriel, and he could see that she was waiting for him to comment.

"Beth's ready," he said emphatically.

"And Peter?"

"He's ready, too."

"He isn't fifty, living with his parents and unemployed, is he? Or…married?"

Gabriel shook his head. "No, he's single and he has a good position at the home office of Starbucks. He's doing well financially and is popular with his peers."

"Just like Beth."

"Beth's resisted opening herself to love," Gabriel said. As for this new relationship—well, there were a few facts yet to be uncovered, facts Goodness would have to learn on her own.

"Beth needs to be taught that she's capable of falling in love again," Goodness murmured.

"Yes," Gabriel said, encouraging her as much as he dared.

"Peter might not be the one, though."

He wasn't sure what Goodness had against the young man. "That's not up to us," he said sternly.

"Right." Goodness folded her hands. "I'll do my best to steer them toward each other. After that, they'll have to work it out for themselves."

Gabriel squinted at her. She sounded as though she was reciting something she'd memorized. "I'm relying on you," he reminded her. "You need to be very clear about your own boundaries. You're there to help them, Goodness, to give them a nudge—not to push them into each other's arms."

"I won't let you down," she promised.

Gabriel sincerely hoped that was true. Just as he was about to expand on his concerns, another urgent prayer request whisked past him, landing on his desk.

Gabriel sighed as he bent to read this one. It came from nine-year-old Carter Jackson. Ah, yes. This wasn't the first time he'd heard from the young man. Carter wanted a dog. He decided to assign Shirley to this request, since she had a particular affinity for children.

Shirley, Goodness and Mercy back on earth. If his hair wasn't already white, that would've done it.

5

Carter Jackson pressed his ear as hard as he could against his bedroom door. If he shut his eyes and concentrated he could hear his parents' conversation.

"I'm sorry, honey. I know how much Carter wants a dog, but we can't afford one right now."

"But, David, we promised."

"I didn't promise him any such thing, Laurie. I said *maybe* he could have a dog for Christmas."

Carter's mother sounded sad. "It'll break his heart."

"Believe me, I know that. I don't like this any better than you do."

Although he was only nine, Carter understood that his father wanted him to have a dog, just as he had when he was Carter's age. Carter had already decided to give his dog the same name as his father's—Rusty. Rusty was a good name for a dog.

"We could get a dog from the shelter," his mom was saying. "A rescue."

"It's not the cost of the dog. It's the vet bills, the food, everything else."

His mother didn't respond.

"You looked at the budget, didn't you? If there was any way we could make it happen, we would. But you know as well as I do that we can't afford a dog. We can barely afford a Christmas tree!"

Carter wasn't sure what a budget was, but he knew it must have something to do with money. Money always seemed to be a problem. His mother used to work at a dress shop in downtown Leavenworth, but the shop closed and she hadn't been able to find another job.

That was all right with Carter. He liked having her at home, and so did his little sister, Bailey. After school they both liked being able to go home rather than to the day care lady down the street. Their mother usually had a snack or a small surprise waiting for them. She seemed happier, too, not to be working such long hours, but Carter knew there were problems with the budget...whatever that was.

"Our health insurance rates just went up," his father said.

"I saw that," his mother murmured. Her voice was quiet, making it difficult for Carter to hear everything she said. "I try to keep the heat as low as I can while the kids are in school, not that it's helped all that much."

That explained why his mother was always wearing a sweater when Carter got home from school.

"The oil prices are killing us," his father said. He sounded angry.

"I know. I'm sorry." This came from his mother.

"It's not your fault, Laurie."

Carter risked opening the door a crack, to see what

he could. It took a moment for his eyes to adjust to the light, but then he saw his parents. They sat on the sofa and his mother's head rested on his father's shoulder. His father had one arm around his mother, and they seemed to be leaning against each other.

"Should we tell Carter now or wait until Christmas morning?" she asked.

Carter bit his lip. They'd *promised* him a dog. His father said he hadn't, but he *had*. He just didn't remember. He'd said it this summer, and ever since then Carter had hung on to that promise—he could have a dog at Christmas.

It wasn't fair and he struggled not to break into tears. Turning his head, he buried his face in his arms and breathed deeply. He couldn't let them see him standing there—or hear him cry.

"I don't think we'll be able to buy the kids any gifts this year," his father continued.

"It's all right, honey," his mother reassured him. "There'll be plenty of presents from your parents and mine. The gifts from your family are already here. The kids will have something to open. Besides, we don't want to spoil Carter and Bailey. It's more important that they know the true meaning of Christmas."

His father seemed to agree.

Carter couldn't listen to any more of their conversation. His sister was sound asleep in the bed across from his own. Bailey was in first grade and he was in fourth. Bailey wanted her own room. But if he couldn't have a dog, then Bailey wasn't going to get a bedroom all to herself, either. That was what Bailey had asked Santa for in her letter.

The kids at school told Bailey she was stupid to believe in Santa. Carter didn't believe anymore, but he didn't want to say anything, especially to his little sister. She still believed. When he was her age, he'd wanted to believe, too.

Santa was like his grandparents who lived in Wenatchee. His mother's family didn't have a budget, or at least he didn't think so. It never seemed hard for them to buy presents the way it was for his parents. Maybe…

Carter decided he'd mention the possibility to his mother in the morning and see what she said. If his own mom and dad couldn't afford a dog, then maybe they'd let his grandparents buy him one. Or perhaps Grandma and Grandpa could pay the vet bills his dad was so worried about.

Feeling better now, Carter pulled back his sheets and slipped into bed. He'd just closed his eyes when a backup plan came to mind. Santa might be make-believe but God was real, and Christmas was Jesus's birthday. Remembering that, he got out of bed and knelt down. He'd already said his bedtime prayers, but this was extra. He hoped God wouldn't mind hearing from him again.

"Dear God," he whispered. "Thank You for Your birthday. I think it's great that because You were born we get presents. I'm really glad You arranged it like that. Um, God, I asked about getting a dog before and my parents said I had to wait. I waited. It was hard, too.

"They said I had to be nine years old before I was responsible enough to take care of a dog. Well, I'm nine and I do all my chores and I do my homework and I don't cheat on tests or anything."

He hesitated, thinking he'd better tell the whole truth. God knew anyway. "Sometimes Mom has to remind me about my chores. But I *try* to be good."

Carter paused, wondering if God might say something back. He listened intently, his eyes closed, but no matter how hard he concentrated he couldn't hear anything. That didn't mean God wasn't listening, though; Carter understood that.

"If You could find a way to get me a dog for Christmas, God, I'd really like it. I promise to take care of Rusty and train him right. I'll make sure he's loved. Thank you."

Finished now, Carter lowered his head and whispered, "Amen." He stayed on his knees a few minutes longer, in case God wanted to talk to him, after all. Eventually he climbed back into bed.

God had a dog for him, a special one. Carter was sure of it. He didn't know how the dog would arrive. Maybe his grandparents would give him one for Christmas, maybe not. He'd just wait and see. He might not believe in Santa anymore, but Carter believed God answered prayers. All he had to do now was be patient.

* * *

"You heard?" Gabriel asked Shirley. The Prayer Ambassador had once worked as a guardian angel and her love for children was the reason he usually assigned Shirley the prayer requests from boys and girls.

"A dog," Shirley repeated.

"There are more important requests, if you prefer," Gabriel said.

"No," came her immediate reply. "I want to help Carter get his dog."

"I thought you would."

"It's just that…"

"Yes?"

"It's just that I could probably take on two or three such requests while I'm on earth," the angel said with utter confidence. "But I know why you haven't given me more than one."

"You do?" Gabriel asked. "And why would that be?"

"My *real* assignment is to keep watch over Goodness and Mercy. Heaven knows, and I don't mean that as a pun—" she paused and gave him a smug smile "—those two need looking after."

"Indeed they do," Gabriel agreed. "But it seems to me that you've taken part in their schemes a number of times."

"Under protest," Shirley rushed to explain. "I knew they were headed for trouble and I tried to warn them, but they wouldn't listen to me. So what choice did I have?" She shook her head ruefully. "You can't imagine the trouble I've saved you on other assignments. But I'm only one angel and there's only so much I can do on my own."

Gabriel didn't need a reminder of the problems these three had caused. Yes, he did expect Shirley to be a supervisor of sorts for the other two, but as often as not they'd led *her* into temptation. Still…

"As the most responsible of the trio—"

"That would be me," Shirley said, cutting him off. She folded her wings close to her back without revealing any degree of eagerness as Goodness and Mercy had done. Shirley was the picture of calm serenity, of unquestionable confidence.

"Let me point out the time limitations involved," Gabriel said. "All three of you need to return to heaven on Christmas Eve." This shouldn't come as any surprise, since it was one of the terms always set upon them during visits to earth at this time of year.

A look of panic flashed into Shirley's eyes. "That means we have barely a week by the earthly calendar."

"Don't forget, we need you back for the festivities," Gabriel told her.

"Yes, of course." She did seem unusually concerned with the temporal constraints, which he found odd, considering that they'd answered prayer requests in less time than that.

"If there are problems, I can come directly to you?" Shirley asked.

It went without saying that with Goodness and Mercy, there were bound to be problems. "Of course."

On second thought, Gabriel wasn't so sure of that. He'd seen compassion and a new depth in Mercy; she understood the seriousness of her assignment. Harry Alderwood's days on earth were few, and Mercy would have to convince Rosalie to move and at the same time prepare Harry for the crossing. Heaven awaited his arrival.

As far as Goodness went... That was an entirely different story. Beth Fischer had lessons to learn, obstacles to negotiate—obstacles of her own making. It might not be as easy as Goodness assumed to steer her toward the future. Gabriel would keep a close eye on this assignment.

And young Carter Jackson—this wasn't an easy prayer request, either, despite what Shirley seemed to think. She might be a relatively senior angel, but she had a few lessons to learn herself.

"Can I see Carter?" Shirley asked.

"Of course." As he'd done with the others, Gabriel parted the veil between the two realms and offered Shirley a chance to assess the situation.

Sitting at the breakfast table, Carter watched his parents closely.

"You remember this summer you said I could have a dog when I'm nine, Dad?" he asked, braving the subject dearest to his heart.

His dad exchanged a look with his mother. "I remember."

"I'm nine now."

His father put down his fork, and the careful way he laid it on the table told Carter this was going to be an important discussion. "Son, it hurts me to tell you this, but we can't afford a dog."

"Dad…"

"I'm sorry. I know you've been hoping to get a dog, but we can't manage it financially, Carter."

Despite his efforts, Carter's eyes filled with tears and everything in the room went blurry. His mother came to stand behind him. Embarrassed to be caught crying, Carter wiped his face with his sleeve and gulped several times.

"As soon as we can afford one, we'll get you a dog," she whispered, placing her hands on his shoulders. "We promise."

"But you promised *before*," Carter challenged. "You said I could have a dog when I turned nine. And then you said I had to wait until Christmas. And now…"

His father looked as sad as Carter had ever seen him. "I'm sorry, Carter. I'm doing the best I can, and so is your mother."

Bailey had started to cry, too. Carter tried to stop, but all he could do was sniffle back the tears. He felt like running away from the table. He couldn't eat.

"What about Grandma and Grandpa Parker?" he asked, clinging to the dream that his grandparents would give him the dog he so badly wanted.

"I've spoken to them," his father said.

Carter felt hope spring to life as he held his breath, waiting to hear the verdict.

"If your grandparents buy you a dog, that's just the beginning of what it'll cost. There's a whole lot more that goes along with owning a dog."

"He could eat my food," Carter insisted. He'd already considered this. "I don't mind sharing."

"Then there are shots."

"I'll take them," Carter said. It didn't matter how much they hurt, either.

"The shots are for the dog, Carter, and they're expensive."

"Oh."

"There's the license and obedience school and neutering and a dozen other costs. All of that would drain the family budget. It won't be long, though. Okay?"

Carter wasn't sure he should believe his father. "How long?"

"David." His mother's voice was soft and filled with warning, almost as if she feared his father would make another promise he couldn't keep.

"I don't know, but I promise that as soon as we can afford it, you'll get your dog."

That was the same thing his mother had said. Carter swallowed hard. He couldn't ask his father's parents. They lived back east and they mailed their gifts, which had arrived last week. The gaily wrapped presents were arranged on the coffee table with a miniature Christmas tree his mother had bought at the grocery store for five dollars. His one hope had been Grandma and Grandpa Parker—his mom's parents—and according to his father, it wasn't going to happen.

His last chance, his only chance now, was God. And with everything inside him, Carter believed God would send him a dog.

"Me, too." Rosalie didn't drive. His own abilities were severely limited now and he took to the road only when necessary. In fact, he hadn't driven since he'd gone to see the doctor on Monday. The days of Sunday-afternoon excursions into the country had long since passed.

One of the advantages of shopping on Wednesday mornings was the lack of crowds. Mostly it was a few folks like Rosalie and him. Recently the store had gotten motorized carts for handicapped and elderly patrons, which made the whole experience a lot more pleasant.

Harry drove the motorized cart while his wife strolled by his side, filling the basket. Not once in the past year had Rosalie complained about the fact that he was the one who wrote their grocery lists, a chore she used to do.

They'd just turned down the soup and canned vegetable aisle when Lucy Menard entered from the other end. Her face brightened as soon as she saw them.

"Rosalie," Lucy called out. She left her own cart and hurried toward her friend, arms wide open.

6

Rosalie Alderwood was humming "O Come, All Ye Faithful" in the kitchen while Harry watched the news on TV. This was Wednesday, their traditional shopping day, and the advertised grocery specials were in the morning paper. Soup was on special, tomato, his favorite, two cans for a dollar. So was ice cream—three half-gallons for only six dollars. The brand wasn't his favorite but ice cream was ice cream, and Harry had always had a weakness for it. He didn't have much appetite anymore, but the thought of chocolate ice cream was appealing.

For years—ever since his retirement—Harry and Rosalie had done their grocery-shopping in the middle of the week.

"Should I get the car warmed up?" Harry asked. He'd put off the conversation with his daughters about selling it; maybe he'd call them tonight.

"Good idea." Rosalie came to stand in front of him, a dish towel in her hand, and glanced at the advertisements in the paper, spread out on the coffee table.

"You'll want to get a few cans of the tomato soup that's on special," he said.

"Yes," she agreed.

Because Rosalie had gotten so absentminded, Harry had begun compiling lists of items they needed to pick up at the store. This morning they were out of both milk and bread. He didn't want to miss that ice cream, either. He planned to arrive early enough to have his selection of fresh flowers, too. Maybe a potted poinsettia in honor of the season... His pleasures were few.

"I'll get my coat," Rosalie told him.

Harry nodded and reached for his car keys hanging on the peg by the door. She left, and knowing Rosalie, it would take her ten minutes to get ready. And that was *after* telling him to start the car. Early on in their marriage, that habit used to irritate him, but not anymore. This tendency to dawdle was part of Rosalie's personality and Harry had learned to accept it.

Before he went out to the car, he checked the refrigerator.

Another of Rosalie's longtime habits was her inability to discard things, even rotting food. He didn't understand it but had realized years ago that he was the one who'd have to toss the leftovers. Thankfully, with her cooking so little, there wasn't much. A quick inspection of the contents revealed several odd items. Frankly Harry had no idea why they needed anchovy paste or five varieties of mustard. Good grief, he hadn't even known they *made* that many.

Sure enough, it was ten minutes before Rosalie appeared. She'd put on fresh lipstick and combed her hair. "I'm ready, Harry."

The two women hugged for an extra-long moment. During World War II, after Rosalie and Harry were married and while he was off fighting in Europe, she and Lucy had roomed together while working in the Portland, Oregon shipyards. At one time, they'd been as close as sisters. In fact, Lucy was godmother to their oldest daughter, Lorraine. Ever since Jake, Lucy's husband, had died, they hadn't seen much of her, which was sad. Mostly Harry blamed himself. Getting out and about was so difficult these days....

"I swear it's been a month of Sundays since I saw you two," Lucy said, stepping back. She looked good, better than the last time Harry had seen her, which was...well, no wonder. It'd been at Jake's funeral.

"I've been meaning to let you know I've moved," Lucy said excitedly.

"Moved?" Rosalie seemed to find that hard to believe.

Lucy beamed. "The kids finally convinced me that with Jake gone, I shouldn't be living on my own."

"I'm surprised you'd leave your home," Rosalie murmured. She glanced at Harry, then looked away.

If it was up to Rosalie she'd delay moving as long as possible.

"I got a place at Liberty Orchard, the new assisted-living complex off Frontier Street."

That caught Harry's attention and he instantly straightened.

"Harry's been saying we need to do something like that, too, but I don't think I can," Rosalie admitted sheepishly.

"I said the same thing." Lucy nodded. "I figured after living in the same house for thirty years, I was too old to make that drastic a change. I told my children they were handing me a death sentence, moving me out of my home."

"That's how I feel," Rosalie said, once again avoiding Harry's gaze.

"But you did move," Harry broke in. "And you're happy now, right?"

"Oh, yes." Lucy smiled contentedly. "I always assumed it would take a forklift to get me out of that house. The thought of sorting through and packing up all those years of living just overwhelmed me."

Harry knew that was part of Rosalie's problem, too.
"Thank goodness the kids came in and made all the
decisions for me. They went through each room, packing what I needed and dividing up what I didn't. One
day I was in my home and the next I was making
friends at Liberty Orchard. It's the best thing that's
happened to me in ten years."

Frowning, Rosalie regarded her friend. "Don't they
serve meals there?" she muttered. "Why are you shopping?"

"The meals are great, but a few times a week I don't
feel like being sociable. That's my choice, you know. I
fix myself something to eat. I've got my own refrigerator and microwave and that's all I need." She held
up a box of microwave popcorn and giggled like a
schoolgirl. "I love this stuff."

"It sounds like the ideal setup," Harry said.

"I'm not ready," his wife murmured.

Because Harry recognized her fears, he hoped to reassure her and gently urge her along. "Maybe Rosalie
and I could come and see you at your new digs," he

suggested jauntily, as though he was proposing a casual visit.

His hope was that once Rosalie saw the facilities for herself, she'd have a change of heart. If *he* couldn't get her to tour Liberty Orchard, perhaps Lucy could.

"How about tomorrow afternoon?" Lucy said. "Around three o'clock? We have a book club meeting at two and there's an exercise class before that. I wouldn't want to miss either one."

"They have exercise classes?" Rosalie sounded impressed.

"There's something to do every day. Before the move, it was a big deal just to step outside the house."

Rosalie shared a surprised glance with Harry. "I know what you mean. We'd love to come by, Lucy."

"I'll see you tomorrow, then," Lucy said, looking pleased.

She wasn't nearly as pleased as Harry, though. This couldn't have worked out better had he planned it. Lucy's opportune appearance had led to the next day's visit in the most natural possible way. It was exactly what he'd prayed would happen.

They finished collecting their purchases and by the time they returned to the house Harry needed a nap. The doc had insisted he couldn't carry anything heavier than five pounds, so his wife brought in the groceries from the garage. He made it to his recliner and was asleep almost before he elevated his feet.

Mercy was delighted at how well the meeting with Lucy Menard had gone. She sat in the motorized cart Harry had recently vacated, flushed with pleasure.

"How did you manage *that?*" Goodness asked, sitting on the handlebars of the same cart. "Did you know about Lucy?"

Hands behind her head, Mercy leaned back, gleeful with joy. "I did some research and discovered that Lucy and Rosalie had once been best friends. Then I noticed that she'd recently moved into Liberty Orchard. After that, all I had to do was arrange a coincidental meeting in the grocery."

"And, pray tell, how did this 'coincidental' meeting come about?"

"I simply absconded with her remaining package of

microwave popcorn. I also shuffled around her collection of DVDs and put *It's a Wonderful Life* on top. Which reminded her it's time for her annual viewing—and that, of course, means she needs popcorn." Mercy chortled. "Piece of cake."

"Did someone mention the bakery?" Shirley asked, fluttering down from above, her wings stirring up flyers in the store's foyer. A youngster chased after them, then disappeared into the store.

When Shirley caught sight of Mercy on the motorized cart, her eyes widened. "Don't even think about it," she warned. "Gabriel asked me to keep an eye on the two of you. He knows, as I do, that you aren't to be trusted."

"I wasn't going to take the cart for a spin or anything," Mercy protested.

"But you *did* think about it."

Shirley knew her all too well. "I considered it." Mercy sighed heavily. "But I'm older and wiser now, and no longer given to flights of fancy." This thing was almost as good as a golf cart (there'd been that unfortunate incident at the Augusta golf course) but if Shirley wasn't going to say anything, Mercy certainly wouldn't, either.

"You're not to encourage her," Shirley warned Goodness.

"Moi?" The other angel brought her hand to her heart with an expression of pure innocence.

Shirley claimed the seat on a second cart. "I thought we should confer before we start our assignments," she said.

Mercy didn't know when Shirley had been put in charge or begun sounding so self-important. She obviously saw herself as their boss; this didn't sit right with Mercy, but she'd do whatever it took to finish her assignment.

"We each have an important task set before us," Shirley announced as if standing at a podium and addressing a huge crowd. She tilted her chin upward and spoke in deep, resounding tones. "This is our opportunity to prove ourselves once and for all to Gabriel and—" she paused, seemingly for effect "—to God."

"Gabriel and God," Mercy and Goodness dutifully repeated, their eyes meeting.

"It is our task," Shirley continued righteously, "no, our *duty,* to teach these humans a lesson from our heavenly Father before we answer their prayer requests."

"Our duty," Mercy and Goodness echoed.

At that point, Shirley deigned to actually face them. "You've got that look," she said.

"What look?" Mercy demanded.

"The guilty look that tells me you did something you shouldn't have."

"I haven't," Mercy insisted. "Not that it's any of your business."

"I'm working with Beth Fischer," Goodness said, getting in between the other two. "This isn't an easy assignment. I could use some advice."

"What's the problem?" Shirley's tone was, in Mercy's opinion, more than a bit condescending.

Goodness frowned meaningfully before she explained. "It appears that Beth's confidence in her ability to choose a life partner has been badly shaken. She doesn't trust her heart."

"Why is that?" Shirley asked.

"I don't know for sure. I've been watching and

studying Beth, and she's a wonderful woman. It's just that…that…" She hesitated. "It's just that I'm afraid she's still in love with her ex-husband. How am I supposed to help her get over him and involved with someone else in only one week? It's *impossible*."

Mercy could understand her friend's dilemma. "Didn't you tell me her ex has remarried?"

"Yes."

"Then you need to teach her to let go," Shirley said unequivocally. "This happens all the time. It's been almost ten years and she has to move on."

"I agree, but it's going to be difficult to convince Beth of that. Thanks for the advice, though." To Mercy's ear, Goodness sounded a little—just a little—sarcastic.

"I'll help you," Shirley said.

"No," Goodness returned immediately. "I appreciate the offer, but I can handle Beth on my own. She'll be in Leavenworth this weekend."

"Really?" Shirley moved her hand to her chin in a thoughtful gesture.

"Her friend Heidi invited her to come here for the

Christmas festivities. No town does it better than Leavenworth—or so I've heard."

"What about your assignment?" Mercy asked, directing the question to Shirley.

For the first time, the other angel seemed unsettled. "Yes, well, my assignment is deceptively simple—on the outside."

"I don't believe you mentioned whose request you've been sent to answer."

"It's a boy named Carter," Shirley mumbled. "He wants a dog for Christmas."

Mercy swallowed a protest. *She* was dealing with a dying old man who had pressing concerns for his family. Goodness had to guide a young woman with a broken heart. And all Shirley had to do was find a little boy a dog! Talk about easy! Mercy could manage that with one wing tied behind her back.

"As I explained, my assignment is deceptively simple, but—"

"Yes, deceptively." Mercy looked at Goodness. "Listen, I'd love to stay and chat awhile, but I've got work to do."

"Me, too," Goodness said.

"Yes, well, Carter and his sister are in school, so I've got a few minutes to spare," Shirley informed her friends.

"I'm sure you do," Mercy said and promptly disappeared. Goodness followed, leaving Shirley sitting alone in the grocery foyer.

A minute later, Mercy returned, hovering behind Shirley, who hadn't moved from her position on the motorized grocery cart. Shirley seemed to assume the other two had left the premises, and Mercy let her think that. She studied the cart for a moment. These little numbers were a breeze to operate. Not that Shirley, so righteous and well-behaved, would know that.... With the lightest touch of her finger, Mercy fired the cart's engine to life.

Stunned, Shirley glanced around, obviously wondering what had changed and why. Mercy wasn't about to tell her. The cart took off into the store with Shirley on board.

Shoppers gasped and leaped out of the way. Several people reached for their cell phones to snap pictures of the runaway cart, careering through the store minus a rider.

Mercy covered her mouth to hold back a laugh. Goodness joined her, laughing, too. Shirley wasn't nearly so calm.

"Mercy!" she screamed. "Help! Do something."

"I believe she already did." Goodness chuckled and disappeared once again. Mercy did, too. Since Shirley had time on her hands, she could use it figuring out how to turn off the cart.

7

Beth wasn't imagining it. The relationship between her and Peter had shifted since the night of her mother's call. That'd been two days ago, and whenever they logged on to the game she lowered her guard a fraction more. So did Peter.

The biggest difference was that they chatted far more than strictly necessary. And their messaging didn't concern the game as much as it did each other.

You're right on time, I notice, he wrote when she logged on.

Beth kicked off her shoes as she settled into the chair by her desk. She set aside the soda she was drinking in order to respond. **You're ahead of schedule.**

I was anxious.

Beth read his words and leaned away from her desk. She wasn't sure how to decipher that comment. Did Peter mean he was anticipating her arrival? Or was he implying that he was worried she'd be late? It was hard to tell.

Anxious why? she asked, preferring the direct approach.

To talk to you.

Now that they'd reached level forty in World of Warcraft, the option to purchase a mount had been offered to them. It was a big advantage and one they'd been considering. **Any particular reason?** she asked, wondering if that was what he wanted to discuss.

Yeah.

That didn't tell her anything. **Would you care to explain?**

His reply didn't come for a couple of minutes, as if he needed to think about it first. So this obviously wasn't about the possibility of adding a mount to their list of resources.

We've been partners—how long? he asked instead.

Six months.

It seems longer.

Again Beth didn't know what to make of that. **Really?**

I trust you.

She laughed. **As well you should. I've covered your butt often enough, oh mighty Timixie.**

I've covered yours, too.

For which I'm most grateful.

That's only appropriate.

Beth laughed, enjoying the light, teasing quality of their exchange. She typed quickly. **Are you going to chatter all night or are we going to play?**

Can't we do both?

Beth felt a rush of warmth. It was a pleasant sensation and one she'd almost forgotten. Talking with the opposite sex was awkward for her, except in situations that didn't involve potentially romantic expectations—with family, for instance, or male colleagues or friends like Sam. She felt comfortable with Peter, at ease. Although they hadn't even spoken on the phone, let alone face-to-face, it was the first time she'd had that kind of reaction to a man since John.

Despite what her mother said, Beth *had* dated after her divorce; she just hadn't done it successfully. Most social conversations with men felt stilted. She struggled with how much to say or not to say.

Her record was three dates with the same man. Luke Whitcomb. He'd been a nice guy, entertaining and funny. His sense of humor had carried her for the three dates.

She probably would've accepted a fourth except that he'd admitted their relationship wasn't working for him. He'd been sincere when he said they should call it quits before either of them got hurt.

Well, surprise, surprise. Luke's rejection had cut deep and served, once again, to convince Beth that she was incapable of ever attracting another man. Afterward she'd steered away from dating at all and a couple of weeks later, she'd found the World of Warcraft and since then, almost her entire social life had been as a Night Elf and hunter.

Now there was Peter, a man she'd never actually met. His family had suggested he "get a life," so it was highly probably that he was single, too. Beth wanted to ask him, only she couldn't figure out how to do it without being obvious. A straightforward question about his marital status seemed out of line at this stage.

They'd been into the game for about ten minutes when Peter sent her another message. **This might be a stupid question but are you...single, married, whatever?**

He'd asked *her.*

Beth's relief was instantaneous. **Single.**

Me, too.

Age?

Is this an interrogation? she typed back.

Sort of. Do you mind?

Not really. She didn't, because in the process she was learning more about him.

I'll tell if you will.

All right.

I'm edging toward thirty, he typed. **Which is one reason my family is after me to meet someone.**

Me, too. Her heart really started to pound then. Perhaps that candle her mother had lit in church was working. Perhaps, in some quirky way, her prayer had taken effect.

Peter was single; she was single.

He lived in Seattle and she lived in Seattle.

He was close to her age and a professional, just as she was.

This almost sounded too good to be true.

My family says it's time I met someone, she typed next.

They do? He seemed as astonished as she felt—as if he, too, was finding this a bit too coincidental. Eerie, even.

A moment later, he typed, **What's wrong with you?**

Well, he was direct enough, but she'd been pretty honest with him, too. She toyed with the idea of telling him she'd been married and divorced, and then remembered Heidi's advice. It wasn't necessary to blurt out everything on the first date—even if this wasn't exactly a date.

I spend too much time playing computer games.

She smiled as her fingers skipped effortlessly over the keyboard.

I've got the same problem, came his reply.

Silly though it was, Beth felt sure they were both smiling. Their conversation went on for another hour, and she was shocked to realize the game had become secondary.

That night when Beth crawled into bed and drew the blanket over her shoulders, she fell into an easy, peaceful sleep. She woke with a feeling of expectation, as if something wonderful was about to happen. Keeping her eyes closed, she tried to hang on to that sensation for as long as she could, afraid reality would chase it away.

The phone rang while she dressed for work. Call display told her it was her mother.

"Hi, Mom," she said, answering the phone while fastening an earring.

"You sound happy."

"I am—well, kind of."

Her mother's hesitation was brief. "Does this have anything to do with the man you met on that computer game you're always playing?"

Beth found it hard to believe she'd actually mentioned Peter to her mother. She'd done it on impulse—a bad impulse—hoping to shut down a barrage of veiled criticism and heavy-handed encouragement. Normally her mother would be the last person she'd tell. "We haven't even met, Mom," she finally confessed. "At least not in the flesh."

"What's the holdup?"

"He hasn't suggested we meet outside the game," Beth said, which in her opinion was a perfectly logical explanation. In her mother's generation, the men always did the asking. She figured this was an excuse even her marriage-obsessed mother would accept.

"Then *you* suggest it."

So much for that. "Mother!"

"I'm serious," Joyce said. "Why beat around the bush? You're a woman who knows what she wants. Now go and get it."

Beth thought about asking Peter. Why not? One of them had to break the ice. "I'd like to meet him but I don't want to appear forward."

"Marybeth, you don't have much time. Maybe he's

shy. Maybe he's waiting for you to bring it up. Show a bit of initiative, will you? It's later than you think."

"Trust me, Mother, Peter isn't shy." She knew this from the way he attacked their enemies on WoW.

"Then why wait?"

Beth nibbled on her lower lip. "I don't want to rush into anything."

"But it's already December twentieth. Christmas is right around the corner."

This wasn't making sense. "Why is it so important that Peter join us for Christmas?" Beth asked, beginning to have some suspicions.

"It isn't important... Well, in a manner of speaking it is. Your father and I have this wager."

"Mother!" Her parents constantly made small bets with each other. Most of the time Beth found this habit of theirs amusing. Not now, though. Not when their wager was about *her*. "You'd better tell me everything."

"Okay..." Her mother inhaled deeply. "Last Christmas, your father said that at the rate you were going you'd never remarry."

"And you disagreed with him."

"Of course I did! Marybeth, you have no idea what an attractive young woman you are. You should be happy."

"I am happy," she insisted.

"I disagree. You just think you are."

Beth rolled her eyes, knowing it wouldn't do any good to argue.

"You should be dating," her mother continued.

"And getting married and becoming a mother." The litany was a familiar one.

"Yes," Joyce Fischer said. "I hate the idea that you've got nothing more pressing to go home to than that darned computer game."

"You don't understand, Mom. Peter and I are at level forty and—" She stopped. There was no point in explaining further.

"I beg your pardon?"

"Never mind."

"Does this have anything to do with bringing Peter to dinner on Christmas Day?" her mother wanted to know.

"Nothing whatsoever."

"But that's the important thing here. Otherwise your father..."

"Yes?" Beth murmured.

"Otherwise I'll be hauling the garbage out to the curb every Wednesday for the next six months."

"A fate worse than death," Beth muttered sarcastically.

"It isn't that I mind dealing with the garbage," her mother went on, "but I do mind losing another bet to your father, especially when you're so close to actually having a date for Christmas."

Beth didn't consider herself close at all. In her desperation to win this bet, Joyce was being completely unreasonable.

"Promise me you'll ask Peter," her mother pleaded.

This had gone on long enough. "I'll do no such thing."

"If not for my sake, then your own, Marybeth."

"No!" That was final, too.

The silence that followed weakened her resolve. "Don't you realize how ridiculous you're being?" Beth said. "Peter's practically a stranger."

"Just meet him," Joyce wheedled. "That's all I ask. Whether he comes to Christmas dinner or not is entirely up to you. All I ask is that the two of you connect. Promise me that much."

While she'd never openly admit it, Beth was curious about her online partner. She couldn't help it. She wondered if he was being pressured by his family about meeting her, too. It was worth asking.

She ended the conversation with her mother by booking a lunch date for later in the week.

That evening, as soon as Beth got home from work, she logged on to the game. Peter came on ten minutes after that. The first thing he did was ask about the amount of gold they'd accumulated toward their purchase of a mount. The fact that he avoided the kind of personal comment they'd exchanged the night before was telling. She suspected he was uncomfortable with the way their conversation had turned toward the personal. It had unsettled her, too, and at the same time excited her.

Beth took his cue and simply answered his question.

They played for an hour, but neither one seemed focused on the game.

I need to leave early, she typed in.

Do you have a hot date?

It wasn't a date at all. Beth was meeting Heidi to go over the details of their weekend in Leavenworth. **An appointment,** she told him.

Business or pleasure?

He was getting mighty inquisitive. **Pleasure,** she answered.

There was a slight pause. **Have fun.**

You, too.

No problem meeting tomorrow night?

He'd never asked before. **None.**

Good. Talk to you then.

Beth put Borincana safely away and exited the game. The happy feeling that had greeted her that morning had completely evaporated. She didn't understand what had happened with Peter or why. Was he backing off, losing interest? He'd been eager to confirm that she'd be playing tomorrow, though, so he might just prefer his romance virtual. He might be afraid of taking their relationship into the realms of reality.

What a sorry lot they were, both of them more comfortable in the guise of a fantasy character than dealing with real life. They were two sad, lonely people reaching out at Christmas, wanting to connect and too afraid to try.

8

Carter waited at the bus stop with his sister and stamped his feet to ward off the cold. With only two school days—including today—left before winter break, everyone was talking about Christmas and what they expected to find under the tree. Carter knew that his parents couldn't afford gifts. Still, there were several wrapped ones from his grandparents that his mother had already set out. Their Christmas tree was pitiful, but he didn't care as long as there were presents. He just hoped all of his weren't socks or underwear.

As the big yellow bus belched to a stop, Carter grabbed his sister's hand. His mother had instructed him to look out for Bailey, and Carter took his duties seriously.

The bus doors slid open and Carter pushed Bailey ahead of him. As he climbed the steps and felt the warm air on his face, he pulled off his woolen mittens, stuffing them in his pockets. Bailey raced down the aisle toward her friend, Maddy. Ignoring her now, Carter took a seat next to his best friend, Timmy Anderson.

"Want to trade lunches?" Timmy asked. Carter tried to remember what his mother had packed in his *Pirates of the Caribbean* lunch pail. She'd baked cookies the night before and there was the usual peanut-butter-and-jelly sandwich, plus an apple. He had an apple every day, no matter what. Timmy did, too.

"What you got?" Carter asked.

Timmy opened his *Spider-Man* lunch box. "Potato chips, a Twinkie, a pudding cup and an apple."

"No sandwich?"

Timmy shook his head.

Timmy's lunch was filled with all the treats Carter only got if he traded. He loved Twinkies, but his mother baked really good chocolate chip cookies.

"Well?" Timmy pressed. "Wanna trade or not?"

"Okay."

The two boys switched lunch pails. Timmy seemed to like Carter's lunches better than his own. He wanted to trade almost every day.

The bus made another stop and three more students got on. Cameron and Isaiah Benedict came aboard, scrambling into the seat in front of Timmy and Carter.

Cameron twisted around and excitedly announced, "I'm getting an Xbox 360 for Christmas!"

"No way," Timmy said, eyes wide with awe and envy. "I put one on my list, but my parents said it was too expensive."

"Do you know for sure?" Carter asked. He'd thought he was getting a dog like his parents had promised, and that wasn't going to happen. He'd bet Cameron only *thought* he was getting the Xbox.

"Because Mom said if that's what I wanted, I wouldn't get anything else."

"And Cameron's just got one gift under the tree," his younger brother, Isaiah, explained.

"It could be underwear."

Cameron glared at Carter. "That's not funny."

"I'm getting a PSP," Timmy said.

Carter knew that was a PlayStation Portable, a handheld game everyone wanted. "That's great."

The other boys looked at Carter. "What are you getting for Christmas?"

He shrugged, reluctant to tell his friends that his parents had told him he couldn't have the one and only gift he'd ever truly wanted.

"Well, what did you ask for?" Isaiah leaned over the back of his seat.

Carter would've liked a computer and an Xbox, too, but his family couldn't afford those things. He hung his head and whispered, "I asked for a dog." Instantly a lump filled his throat.

"What kind of dog?"

Carter wasn't picky. "A red dog," he said. If he was going to name him Rusty, then he figured the dog should have reddish fur. "Medium size so he can run and fetch and do stuff like that."

His Grandma Parker had a small, yappy dog, a miniature poodle. Suzette was a good pet for his grandmother, but that wasn't the kind of dog Carter had in mind. His dog would play outside with him during the day, after school and on weekends. At night he could sleep in Carter's room on the rug next to his bed. That was what dogs did. They slept by their masters. Rusty would sleep in the very same spot where Carter had gotten down on his knees and prayed.

If he closed his eyes, Carter could picture his dog with big, floppy ears and a tongue that hung out the side of his mouth when he'd been running. Oh, and Carter wanted a boy dog. A girl dog would be all right, too, but he preferred a boy.

"Are you going to get one?" Cameron asked.

Carter hesitated. "I won't know until Christmas," he muttered.

"Your parents are gonna make you wait?"

He nodded rather than admit the truth.

"I wish I'd asked for a dog," Timmy said, sitting dejectedly back in his seat.

"I'll share Rusty with you," Carter offered, and then remembered there wasn't going to be a Rusty.

"You will?"

"Sure," Carter assured his friend.

Timmy gave Carter a gap-toothed grin, and when the bus arrived at school, the two boys hurried off together.

Their teacher stood in the hallway outside their classroom. As they approached, Timmy burst out, "Ms. Jensen, Ms. Jensen! Guess what? Carter's getting a dog for Christmas."

Their teacher's eyes lit up at the news. "Why, Carter, that's wonderful. Do you have a name for him yet?"

"Rusty."

She nodded approvingly. "That's a great name for a dog."

Carter tried to smile but a funny feeling in the pit of his stomach started to bother him. He didn't know what he was going to do once his friends discovered he didn't get Rusty, after all. He should never have said anything to Timmy.

"Carter said he'd let me play with his dog."

Ms. Jensen beamed at him. "It's good to share. I'm

proud of you, Carter." With that, she turned into the classroom and left the two of them waiting in the hallway.

All during their arithmetic lesson, Carter's thoughts wandered to what his friends would say after Christmas when he didn't have his dog. He never should've lied. His stomach hurt the way it always did when he hadn't told the truth.

At recess, Carter walked up to his teacher's desk, holding his stomach. He rarely missed school. In fact, he hadn't stayed home a single day.

"Aren't you feeling well, Carter?" Ms. Jensen asked in a soft caring voice that reminded him of his mother's.

"I have a stomachache."

She pressed the back of her hand against his forehead, then took him down to the nurse's office. Mrs. Weaver was about the same age as his grandmother and had hair that was completely white. She spoke soothingly as she took his temperature. After she'd finished looking at the thermometer, she said he didn't have a fever and suggested he lie down on the couch for a little while.

Carter tried to sleep but he couldn't stop thinking. After a few minutes he sat up, gazing idly out the office window—and that was when he saw it.

A dog.

Outside in the schoolyard was a dog just like the one Carter had imagined. A dog with big, floppy ears. He was exactly the right size, and he jumped and leaped at the students and then chased after a ball. He was skinny and dirty, but Carter could tell that he was a good dog.

He was exactly the kind of dog Carter wanted, although this one didn't have red fur. It was dark and his plumy tail was clumped with mud, but that didn't stop him from wagging it furiously. Watching the other kids play with him made Carter's stomach stop hurting.

"I couldn't reach your mother," Mrs. Weaver told him when she returned.

"I feel better now," he murmured.

"Would you like to go back to your classroom?"

Carter nodded just as the bell ending recess rang. If the dog was still on the playground at lunchtime, Carter would play with him. A sense of exhilaration filled him and he could hardly wait for the midday break.

Carter ate his lunch in record time, then raced outside to the playground without bothering to button up his coat. He'd left Timmy discussing Christmas plans with Isaiah—and enjoying his chocolate chip cookies. The cold, sharp air hit him right in the face, but he didn't care. There weren't many kids outside, but the mutt was there, walking around the yard, sniffing, his nose to the ground. When he saw Carter, the dog instantly ran toward him, looking up with dark pleading eyes.

"Hi, boy," Carter said and dropped to one knee. He withdrew the Twinkie from his pocket, pulled it from its wrapper and fed it to the dog.

The mutt ate the Twinkie in two bites. The poor thing was starved. Now Carter wished he hadn't eaten any of his lunch. He wished he had more food to give his new friend. Thinking quickly, he hurried back into the school. His sister had complained that morning about *another* peanut-butter-and-jelly sandwich. If she didn't want it, Carter did. Not for himself but for the stray.

As he'd expected, his sister was with her friends. She'd eaten everything in her lunch but the sandwich.

"Bailey," he said, breathless now. "Can I have your sandwich?"

Bailey squinted up at him. "What did you do with yours?"

"I gave it to Timmy."

Bailey hesitated. "I was going to eat mine."

"No, you weren't. Come on, Bailey, I need that sandwich."

"What'll you trade me for it?" she asked.

Carter didn't have a lot of time. If he didn't hurry back outside, some other kid would make friends with the dog. He might even leave the schoolyard. "You can watch whatever you want on TV Saturday morning."

His sister's eyes widened. It was a generous offer and she knew it. They only had one television set and their mother made them take turns choosing what to see. Bailey liked sissy stuff, while Carter liked action heroes.

"*All* Saturday morning?"

Carter nodded. With a smug look, Bailey handed over her peanut-butter-and-jelly sandwich.

Grabbing it, Carter hurried back outside. The playground was crowded with kids by then, but as soon as the mutt saw Carter, he bounded across the playground toward him.

Once again, Carter got down on one knee. He wiped the muddy hair from the dog's eyes; his own hands got grimy in the process but Carter didn't care. Taking the sandwich out of his pocket, he tore off the plastic and held it out to the mutt. The bread disappeared as quickly as the Twinkie had.

"You shouldn't be feeding that dog."

Carter glanced up to find Mr. Nicholson, the sixth-grade teacher, who was on schoolyard duty during lunch, scowling down at him. "I've already called Animal Control about this dog once."

"No!" An automatic protest came from Carter. He didn't want this friendly dog to go to a shelter.

"He doesn't belong on the playground."

"He's a nice dog."

Mr. Nicholson didn't agree or disagree. "I don't want to see you feeding him again. Is that understood?"

Carter nodded. The teacher didn't exactly say Carter couldn't feed the stray. What he'd said was that he didn't want to *see* Carter do it.

The teacher went off to intervene in an argument between some sixth-grade kids, and Carter petted the dog's face. "It's all right, boy, I'll bring you food. Will you be here tomorrow?"

The mutt looked back at him with intense brown eyes, as if to say he'd be waiting for Carter.

On his way back to class, Carter washed his hands. He wondered how long the dog had been lost. He sure was dirty, and he seemed lonely, too. Carter's heart ached for him. What the stray needed was a good home and a family, just like everyone did. Carter hoped the Animal Control people didn't catch him before Carter figured out how to bring him to his house.

First he had to explain to his father that this dog wasn't a puppy but a grown-up dog that needed a home. This wasn't an expensive dog, either. He was a plain ordinary dog. He'd probably already had his shots.

That night Carter couldn't keep still at the dinner table. All he could think about was the dog in the schoolyard, out in the cold and dark by himself. He wanted to bring him home right then and there. He was worried the dog might not be safe, or that the people from Animal Control would take him to a shelter. That might not be such a bad thing, because he might be adopted by a family. Except that Carter wanted the dog for himself.

"Carter, eat your dinner," his father said.

Carter stared down at his plate. Spaghetti was one of his favorite meals. His mother had made it specially for him, and all he could do was swirl the noodles around with his fork. He needed to figure out how to smuggle the meatballs off his plate and hide them until morning.

"How were your classes?" his mother asked. It was the same question she asked every night.

"Good," Carter murmured. "I had a tummy ache but it went away."

"Carter fed a dog in the schoolyard and got in trouble." Bailey could hardly wait to tattle on him.

From across the table, Carter glared at his sister.

His father frowned. "Whose dog was it?"

Carter shrugged. "He doesn't belong to anyone."

"He's a stray?"

Carter stared at his plate again. "I guess so."

"He was real dirty and had mud all over him and Carter gave him a sandwich and petted him until Mr. Nicholson made him stop."

"Oh, Carter," his mother whispered.

His father shook his head. "I don't want you bringing that dog home, Carter. Is that understood?"

"Okay."

"I mean it," he said sternly.

Carter swallowed hard as he tried not to cry. "May I be excused, please?" he asked.

His mother gently rested her hand on his. "Yes, you may."

Carter went into the bedroom he shared with his

sister and fell, fully dressed, across his bed. He buried his face in his pillow, praying the dog would still be there the following day.

9

Mercy regarded Shirley suspiciously, her arms folded, her foot tapping. "You brought that dog to the schoolyard, didn't you?" She pointed at the animal, who lay in the sandbox, head resting on his outstretched paws as he slept.

Shirley sat on the swing at the farthest reaches of the yard and shook her head adamantly. "I most certainly did not. I don't have a clue where that dog came from. Trust me, if I brought a dog into Carter's life, it wouldn't be *that* mangy mutt."

Mercy didn't believe her. "I, for one, find it mighty convenient that a stray dog should show up in the schoolyard today." And besides, she knew Shirley loved animals—despite the scornful way she'd spoken about this dog.

"I agree with Mercy." Goodness came to stand at her side, her foot tapping in an identical tempo.

"Stop looking at me like that," Shirley muttered. "Carter can't have a dog. That decision's already been made. You both know I can't interfere with the chain of command. Carter's father feels bad enough as it is, but he's said in no uncertain terms that his son can't have a dog. Why would I complicate matters?"

"Why would she?" Goodness turned to Mercy.

"I don't know, but like I said, I find this entire situation a little too convenient."

Shirley stepped free of the swing and brushed the snow from her hands. "Speaking of convenient, I think it's very interesting that Beth and Peter appear to be so well-matched."

Goodness raised both arms. "Don't look at me. I

didn't have a thing to do with that. They met online six months ago, remember?"

"Quite right," Mercy confirmed. "And before you mention Harry and Rosalie running into Lucy Menard, I've explained that."

A wistful expression came over Goodness. "I do hope everything works out for Beth and Peter."

"Why shouldn't it?" Shirley asked.

"They're both so stubborn—and so scared. What they need is a good shove in the right direction."

"Goodness!" Shirley's expression was scandalized. "Don't even *think* like that. Our job is to teach these humans a lesson. They have to make their own decisions, find their own way."

"Find their own way?" Mercy didn't mean to sound sarcastic, but she couldn't help it. The evidence was overwhelming; humans were a pathetic bunch. "May I remind you that humans wandered in the desert for forty years on a trip that should've taken three months, tops?"

"Joshua had them march around Jericho seven

times, looking for the main gate to the city," Goodness added, shaking her head.

Shirley frowned. "You both know there were very good reasons for those incidents."

"True, but you have to admit humans don't exactly have an impressive track record."

With a disgruntled look, Shirley was forced to admit the truth.

"Humans need help," Mercy reiterated.

"Our help."

Still Shirley didn't seem convinced. "But Gabriel—"

"Will never find out," Mercy assured her. "We won't be blatant about it—just a nudge or two where it's warranted. If Gabriel's going to place us under earthly time constraints, we need to be inventive."

"Inventive," Goodness echoed. "How do you mean?"

"Well, for one thing, it's obvious that you'll have to step in with Beth and Peter."

"I will?"

"Yes." Mercy didn't understand why *she* had to clarify everything for her fellow Prayer Ambassadors.

"Didn't you tell me they still haven't set a time to meet?"

"Well, yes…"

"And the reason is?"

Goodness shifted uncomfortably. "Well, like I said, they're afraid…."

"Afraid of what?" Mercy asked. "Do you suppose maybe they're afraid of being disillusioned?"

"They could be," Goodness said. "And I agree—they need help. The last time I looked, Beth was depressed. Everything was going so well between her and Peter, and then he closed down for no apparent reason."

"Is there anything you can do about it?"

"I… Yes, of course there is." Her eyes darted from side to side. "Unfortunately, I can't think what it would be at this precise moment, but it'll come to me."

"Shirley." Mercy focused her gaze on the former guardian angel.

"Reporting for duty." She stood military straight, wings neatly folded, feet together. Mercy wondered if Shirley was making fun of her.

"How do you plan to help Carter?" she asked.

Shirley's shoulders sagged with defeat. "I'll make sure the dog's nowhere to be seen when he arrives for school tomorrow."

"You're sure that's the right thing for Carter?" Mercy asked, her own heart aching for the little boy.

Reluctantly Shirley nodded. "His father said he couldn't have a dog, no matter what. I don't have any choice."

All three considered this unfortunate set of circumstances.

"Maybe I could steer Carter's father toward a better-paying job," Shirley suggested.

"That's an idea."

Goodness turned to her. "What's happening with Harry?" she asked.

Ah, yes, Harry and Rosalie. "They visited Lucy Menard earlier this afternoon and got a tour of the assisted-living complex."

"And what happened?" Shirley asked.

"Come with me and let's find out," Mercy invited. Together with her two friends, she descended on the house at 23 Walnut Avenue, where Rosalie and Harry sat across from each other at the dinner table.

* * *

"I was surprised at how many of our friends have moved to Liberty Orchard," Rosalie murmured, gazing down at her bowl of canned chicken stew.

She seemed deep in thought, and that encouraged Harry. The visit had gone even better than he could've expected. Rosalie had met three good friends she'd lost contact with in the last few years. Each one had urged them to make the change and become part of the community at Liberty Orchard.

"Did you notice how most people said they were sorry they hadn't moved into assisted living sooner?" Harry waited for his wife to protest. She hadn't wanted him to know, but he could see that she'd been impressed with the facility.

"What I liked was all the social activities," Rosalie murmured.

Harry agreed. He'd been impressed himself, glad, too, because he felt that after he died Rosalie would have the social contact she needed. A wave of sadness washed over him at the thought of leaving his wife behind. He tried not to dwell on the subject of death, but knowing it was imminent, he couldn't stop thinking about it.

Trying not to appear too enthusiastic about the assisted-living complex, Harry nodded.

"My goodness," Rosalie said happily, "those folks have something going on every day of the week."

Harry nodded again, taking a bite of his stew.

"Did you read the dinner menu?" Rosalie asked him. She'd found it posted outside the dining room and gone over it three or four times. She'd had all kinds of questions for Lucy, too. The midday meal was the main one of the day, with a lighter one served at about five. "Why, they had a choice of two soups *and* a salad, plus fish, chicken or meat loaf. And Lucy said it's different every day!"

"I took a look at it myself," Harry said gently. One thing was certain; the residents at Liberty Orchard weren't eating any of their meals out of a can—unless they chose to. He didn't need to point out the obvious, however.

His wife set down her spoon. "Harry," she began shyly, "I'm not sure if you've noticed, but I'm starting to forget things now and then." The admission came with some hesitation. "I've begun to wonder if one of the reasons is that my mind isn't as active as it used to be."

"Lucy said the same thing happened to her," Harry pointed out, reminding his wife of the conversation earlier in the day. "Do you recall how she said that as soon as she spent time with other people again, she wasn't nearly as forgetful?"

Rosalie thought about this for a moment. "She did, didn't she?"

Harry was cautious about saying too much too soon. Rosalie's eyes had been opened when she'd seen the facility, and it didn't hurt that a number of their friends had already made the move.

"Lucy also said the unit closest to hers is available." He said this casually and waited for a response. While his wife had been chatting with her friends, Harry had met with the administrator to see if they could secure that particular unit. Naturally, he wouldn't make a decision like this without discussing it with Rosalie first, but he was beginning to feel confident that she saw the wisdom of such a move.

Rosalie looked at him the same way she had all those years ago, when they'd considered purchasing this very house. She loved this place and Harry loved her. He would've moved heaven and earth to buy the house she wanted.

"Do you honestly think we should give up our home, Harry?"

He hated that it had come to this. "Like I said, this old place is getting to be too much for me."

Slowly Rosalie lowered her gaze and conceded. "And me."

This was the first time she'd been willing to admit that age had taken a toll on her, too. As far as Harry was concerned, it was a giant leap forward.

"We should ask the girls," she said tentatively.

"Good idea." Their youngest daughter was coming to spend Christmas with them, and Lorraine and family would arrive the day after. Both his daughters agreed with Harry. Like him, they recognized the necessity of this change, even if they hadn't quite grasped its urgency.

Harry knew that if Rosalie discussed the situation

with either Lorraine or Donna, their daughters would reassure her in ways he couldn't. He felt it was only a matter of time. God willing, everything would fall into place....

"I don't want to discuss it again until after Christmas, though," Rosalie insisted. "I won't even talk about moving until the holidays are over."

"But, Rosalie, there's only the one unit," he blurted out. "Unless we give the administrator a security check, someone else might take it."

"Then so be it," she said, missing the point that he'd talked to the administrator without her knowledge.

"Mrs. Goldsmith told me there's another party interested." A sense of dread almost overwhelmed him. If they didn't act quickly, the unit would go to some other couple.

"Of course she told you that," Rosalie said with unshakable confidence. "That's what she's supposed to say. It's a tactic, Harry. You, of all people, should know the things people will say when they're after a sale."

Frustration beat hard against his chest. "But, Rosalie…"

"Harry, sweetheart, don't be so concerned. If we lose this unit, another will come up later."

Without telling her what Dr. Snellgrove had said, Harry had no choice but to agree. "Personally, I'd like this all settled *before* the holidays."

"Do you mind if we wait?" Rosalie asked. "It won't make any difference, will it?"

"I suppose you're right," he said reluctantly. "It doesn't really matter." Only it did, but Harry couldn't find it in his heart to tell her why.

Harry left the table and as much as he hated his walker, he reached for it. The damn thing was a nuisance, but at this stage it was a necessary one.

"The girls could help us move while they're here." He made the suggestion as he settled back into his recliner.

"Not over Christmas, Harry. Please, sweetheart, I don't want to ask that of them."

He nodded. He wouldn't mention it again. Not tonight.

"It doesn't look good," Shirley had the audacity to say.

"Rosalie wants to wait until after Christmas."

Mercy didn't know what to do. "That won't work."

"Why not?" Both her friends turned to face her.

Mercy sighed, more burdened now than ever. "Because Harry will be in heaven by then."

10

Joyce Fischer had found a table at the ultra-busy Nordstrom Café by the time Beth got to the store. As soon as she appeared, her mother waved to catch her attention.

Beth felt wonderful and couldn't have disguised her mood had she tried.

"Hello, Mom," she said, giving her mother a quick hug.

"I took the liberty of ordering for you, dear. I just got two of what we usually order."

"That's fine." Beth only had an hour for lunch and although she would've liked to try something new rather than her standard soup du jour and turkey sandwich, she didn't object.

Taking off her coat, Beth draped it over her chair.

"You're positively glowing. What's going on?" Her mother looked like she was about to rub her hands together in glee. "Is it that young man from the computer game?"

"We're going to meet." Beth wasn't sure how and why the situation had changed. Just as she was losing hope that they'd ever take a chance, Peter had stepped forward. Without understanding why it had happened, she realized that a transformation had taken place.

They'd logged on to play World of Warcraft last night and after a while had started exchanging messages again. In the beginning it wasn't anything special, just their normal chitchat. Then out of the blue Peter had made a startling admission.

"He's divorced," Beth informed her mother.

"Well, dear, so are you."

"I know… That's not the point. Peter and I were talking."

"On the phone?"

"No, no, online. That's the only way we've communicated so far."

Her mother frowned, then decided not to make whatever comment hovered on the tip of her tongue. "Go on," she urged instead. "I want to hear everything."

"Well," Beth said, eager now. "He told me that it's taken him some time to get over the divorce, but he thinks he's ready to move on."

"How long has it been?" her mother asked. "I mean, since his divorce was final."

Beth frowned. Her mother was right; that was an important question. "I didn't ask him."

"You should, dear. If it's been less than a year, it might be best to move slowly and carefully in this relationship." Then, as if she regretted having given advice, she shook her head. "Follow your heart. Don't listen to a thing I say."

Beth thought cynically that this was all part of the

wager her parents had. Her mother didn't care if Peter was the brother of Frankenstein's monster as long as he showed up. "You really want him there for Christmas, don't you?"

Her mother's eyes brightened. "Is there any possibility that might happen?"

Beth shrugged. Despite her mother's bet—and personally she felt Joyce deserved to lose—she'd like it if Peter could spend Christmas with her. She wanted to invite him, but it was a lot to ask of someone she hadn't even met. Everything depended on this weekend.

Her mother waved one hand impatiently. "So you told him you're divorced, too?"

"Yes, of course, and then we both started talking so fast it was hard for my fingers to keep up with my thoughts." Peter had been deeply hurt by his wife, who'd more or less kicked him out of the house and excluded him from her life. It'd been painful and harsh, and he'd taken the breakup of his marriage hard.

Beth understood. She'd experienced the same grief over the death of her own marriage. In the course of their conversation, they'd talked about regrets and all the things they might've done to save their marriages. Based on the few details Peter had divulged, Beth regarded his ex-wife as cold and calculating.

She talked about John in ways she never had with anyone else, including her parents. It was as though a festering blister had burst inside her and she spewed out the devastating pain of her own divorce.

The game was forgotten as they continued talking. It was after midnight when Peter reminded her that they both needed to be at work in the morning. Reluctantly Beth had signed off.

"What else did he say?" her mother asked. "Did you tell him your real name is Marybeth?"

"Hardly," she cried, annoyed that her mother would ask such an inane question. "And don't you tell him, either."

"So you did invite him for Christmas?" Her mother looked pleased beyond measure.

"No…not yet." The optimism Beth felt was a sign of her excitement about the way their relationship was developing. No man had interested her this much since college, when she'd first met John. Peter gave her hope. Maybe this wouldn't go anywhere, but at least she was finally taking a risk. Finally willing to try again.

The server brought their lunches, giving Beth a respite from her mother's relentless questioning. She tasted her cream of broccoli soup, and it took a few minutes for the conversation to return to Peter.

"You do expect to introduce him to your family, don't you?" Her mother smiled expectantly at Beth, the turkey sandwich poised in front of her mouth.

"If things go well." She nodded. "We have a lot in common, Peter and me."

"That's wonderful, dear."

Beth felt the giddy sensation of everything coming together at last. "I never dreamed that after all these months we'd connect the way we have."

"Well?" Her mother paused. "When are you going to meet?" Before Beth could answer, she added, "Soon, I hope."

"Is tomorrow soon enough for you?"

"Saturday? But I thought you were going to Leavenworth with Heidi."

"I am."

"You're meeting Peter there?"

Beth nodded. Peter seemed to be a closet romantic, although she suspected he'd never admit it. He was the one who'd wanted to have this initial meeting right away. He'd mentioned getting together on Saturday for lunch, and Beth had said she'd be in Leavenworth. Undeterred, Peter had suggested meeting there.

"But how will that work when you don't know what he looks like? Good grief, Beth, do you have any idea how crowded that town can get, especially this time of year?"

"We've got it all figured out. Heidi and Sam and I are taking the train with the kids and—"

"Peter will meet you on the train?" her mother broke in.

"Not exactly. The train sold out weeks ago, so Peter's taking the bus. We arrive at eleven and, depending on the weather, he should get in around noon."

"The train's always late."

"Oh, ye of little faith."

"I have a lot of faith," her mother said. "But I happen to be practical, too."

"We took that into consideration, Mother. The bus could be late, too, you know."

"Yes, of course."

"We're meeting by the gazebo in the center of town at four o'clock."

"Why not earlier?" her mother demanded.

Beth sighed. "I'm there to spend the day with Heidi, remember? Besides, if this doesn't work out…"

"Fine," Joyce said dismissively. "But how will you recognize each other?"

Beth described their plan. Peter would be carrying a single long-stemmed red rose and wearing a baseball cap with a Seahawks emblem. She, meanwhile, would be wearing a full-length navy wool coat and a red knit hat and muffler.

They should be able to find each other without difficulty. Then they'd watch the tree-lighting ceremony together. The train was scheduled to depart at six-thirty; his bus would leave shortly after that. They'd spend just a couple of hours in each other's company—a safe length of time whether the meeting went well or not. He hadn't said so, but Beth had the distinct feeling that if this meeting *did* go well, Peter would ask to see her again on Sunday.

"You sound so hopeful," her mother said.

"I am." Beth had a positive feeling about this.

"What if...what if Peter isn't as good-looking as you expect?" She seemed genuinely concerned that this might be a possibility.

"It doesn't matter." John had been drop-dead gorgeous. She'd been the envy of all her friends, and what she'd discovered was that good looks made very little difference. Most important was character. Moral fiber, sense of honor and kindness were far more compelling qualities in Beth's eyes.

"You say that now," her mother warned, "but you might change your mind once you meet him."

"Perhaps." But even as she said it, Beth was convinced that her feelings wouldn't change. If there was anything she'd learned from her divorce, it was that looks could be deceiving. John had been completely self-absorbed, selfish, irresponsible.... It was pointless to rehash his shortcomings, of which there'd been plenty.

They finished their lunch and because she had a few minutes to spare, Beth and her mother did some window-shopping. Seattle was a magical city at Christmastime. Beth loved the festive air—the decorations everywhere, the cheerful crowds, the music. Entertainers sang and played instruments. She and Joyce stopped to listen to a violinist whose rendition of "Silent Night" was exquisite as people bustled to and from stores with their bags and packages. The cold wind stung her face and she glanced up at the sky for any sign of snow. Her step was lighter and for the first time in years she felt a rush of joyful anticipation about Christmas.

Her mother wasn't the only one to notice her improved mood. Lloyd, the attorney who'd introduced her to the World of Warcraft, commented on it when she returned from lunch.

"You seem to be mighty happy about something," he said, smiling at her.

"I am," she responded cryptically.

At closing time, she hurried home. As soon as she was back in her condo, Beth logged online, hoping Peter would be there.

He was.

Did you have a good day? he typed.

Great. What about you?

He didn't reply immediately. **It couldn't have been better,** he eventually wrote. **Thank you for listening while I poured out my woes about my marriage last night. I don't often talk about it. I wouldn't have with you, but in all fairness I felt you needed to know.**

Peter, thank you, she hurriedly typed back. **I can't tell you how freeing it was for me to tell you about my divorce. It's not a subject I bring up lightly. I felt like such a failure when we split up and that feeling never went away.**

I know. That's how I felt when my marriage ended, too.

It seems we have even more in common than we realized, she told him.

I was thinking the same thing.

They chatted for most of an hour until Beth's stom-

ach growled, reminding her that she hadn't eaten dinner. Peter couldn't stay online long because he was
seeing a friend, so they ended their conversation.

It was just as well, because Beth had to call Heidi
and let her friend know there'd been a small change
in plans.

After she reached her, Beth explained that she'd be
seeing Peter in Leavenworth and said she hoped Heidi
didn't mind.

"Mind? Of course I don't mind," Heidi told her. "I
think it's so romantic that you two will meet up there.
All we need now is some snow for the day to be absolutely perfect."

Snow in Santa's Village—that would indeed be mar-
velous.

"I wonder if I'm expecting too much," she said, suddenly anxious.

"How can you help it?" Heidi asked. "He does seem
too good to be true."

No dating service could have set her up with a more
suitable candidate. They agreed on practically everything they'd discussed. In the past week, Beth had

learned that they both read the same books, liked the same kinds of food—Mexican and Chinese—and adored anchovies on Caesar salad but not pizza. Granted, those might be superficial similarities, but unlike John, Peter was responsible and dedicated, both qualities she admired. She knew this from his loyalty to his friends, his seriousness about his career—as a coffee buyer at Starbucks—his affection toward his parents and many other examples she'd gleaned.

Maybe he was too good to be true, as Heidi had said. But Beth's instincts told her that Peter was a man she wanted to know better, a man *worth* knowing better. Not that her instincts had been what you'd call reliable in the past. So, before things went any further, she had to learn if this could become a viable relationship—and there was only one way to find out.

In other words, Beth was counting on their face-to-face meeting to tell her whether these feelings for Peter were real—or just a fantasy concocted during their online adventures.

11

Carter could hardly wait to get to school. As soon as the bus dropped him off he headed for the playground, instead of running into the classroom with Timmy and his other friends. Behind the building, he looked carefully around.

Rusty was nowhere to be seen. His heart sank.

"What are you doing out here?" Timmy asked, chasing after him.

"Nothing," Carter murmured, his shoulders slumping. All night he could barely sleep thinking about the stray. The more he thought about it, the more he realized this wasn't just any dog. This was *his* dog. His Rusty. God had sent him this dog. Rusty was the answer to Carter's prayer.

"Wanna play soccer?" Timmy asked. "I can get Cameron and Isaiah and—"

"No, thanks."

Timmy looked as dejected as Carter felt. "It's cold out here. Let's go inside."

"All right." Timmy followed him off the playground and into the building.

When classes started, he had trouble paying attention to Ms. Jensen. Carter kept wondering what had happened to Rusty. He worried that Animal Control had picked him up, and then worried that they hadn't.

Deep down, Carter knew that if Rusty was at a shelter, he'd at least be out of the cold. And there'd be plenty of food for him. But Carter had brought an extra-big lunch today, just in case.

After the recess bell rang, his friends dashed out the

door, eager to put on their winter clothes and get onto the playground.

"Carter." Ms. Jensen stopped him.

Carter trudged over to his teacher. "Yes, Ms. Jensen?" He thought about asking if she'd seen the stray dog recently, but then he remembered Mr. Nicholson's warning.

"Is everything all right?"

"Yes, Ms. Jensen."

"At home, I mean."

He nodded. He wanted to tell her that his family wasn't getting Christmas presents this year and that he'd lied to his friends. He still felt bad about misleading Timmy. But he didn't want the other kids to know that the only gift under the tree would be underwear from his grandmother.

"You don't seem yourself. Are you feeling well?"

"I'm fine, Ms. Jensen. Can I go outside now?"

"All right. Oh, and thank your mother for the cookies she sent me."

"I will," Carter promised.

As he hurried onto the playground, Carter noticed

that his teacher was still watching him. No sooner was he outside with his friends than he saw Rusty. Carter could hardly breathe, he was so excited.

Rusty saw Carter, too, and even though one of the third-grade girls was offering him a cracker, the dog shot across the schoolyard. Carter knelt down to greet his friend. Rusty licked his face and seemed as happy to see Carter as Carter was to see him. Carter dug inside his pocket for a meatball he'd managed to smuggle out of the refrigerator early that morning. Rusty gobbled it up and looked to Carter for more.

"I'm sorry," Carter told him, and then because he was so ecstatic, he wrapped his arms around the dog. He didn't care that Rusty was filthy or that the sleeves of his winter jacket came away all muddy. His mother would be upset, but even her displeasure was worth the enjoyment Carter received from this special dog.

"We can't let Mr. Nicholson see you," Carter warned, then ran over to where his friends were playing.

Rusty followed Carter wherever he went. When Mr. Nicholson stepped into the yard, the stray quickly and quietly disappeared, just as if he understood.

Carter turned around and looked for him, but Rusty was nowhere in sight. Then he saw that the dog had gone into the trees that separated the schoolyard from the nearby houses.

"Good boy," Carter whispered. Rusty was no dummy. He knew who his friends were—and his enemies.

At lunchtime, Carter only ate his apple. The rest he saved for Rusty. Once again the mutt gobbled the food and gazed up at Carter with bright, shining eyes that revealed his gratitude.

Carter petted Rusty's head, although his hand got really dirty. What would happen to the dog over the holidays, when there was no one at the school? Who'd feed Rusty then? Who'd watch out for him? Carter already knew the answer. No one. After today, school was over for the year, and the yard would remain empty until the first week of January. Rusty could starve by then.

Holding the dog's muddy face between his hands, Carter peered into his deep brown eyes. Disregarding what his father had said, Carter whispered, "Rusty, listen, I need you to follow me home."

The dog blinked and stared back at him intently.

"I take bus number seven. Follow that bus, okay?"

Rusty cocked his head to one side.

Carter didn't know what more he could do. Disconsolate, he tried to accept that the dog wouldn't understand him, no matter how many times he repeated the information. After today, when the bus delivered Carter to his home, it was unlikely he'd ever see Rusty again. Carter couldn't bear to have that happen, but he had to prepare himself for disappointment.

Because it was the last day before winter break, school was dismissed an hour early. While Carter lined up with his friends for bus number seven, he scanned the area for Rusty. Again the dog was nowhere to be seen, and once again Carter's heart fell.

"You wanna come to my house and play video games?" Timmy asked, plopping down on the seat next to Carter.

"No, thanks."

His friend seemed dejected.

"Can I come on Monday?" Carter asked.

"Sure." Timmy perked up right away. "I'll show you all my presents under the tree."

"Okay." Carter tried to smile but it was hard. He was glad that his friend was getting lots of gifts. He wanted gifts, too—stacks and stacks of them. But Carter would give up every single one for Rusty.

God had answered his prayer, Carter told himself, struggling to believe. Rusty *would* find him. God had sent Rusty to that schoolyard and now God would figure out a way to bring him to Carter's house.

The bus stopped, and Cameron and Isaiah got off and ran to their home at the end of the street. Their house was the biggest and nicest in the neighborhood.

The next stop was for Carter and Bailey's block. Grabbing his backpack, Carter felt his heart beating hard. He hoped with all his might that Rusty would find his way. Bus number seven. He'd told Rusty to follow bus number seven. Carter knew it would be a miracle if the dog had understood him, but God was in charge of miracles, and He'd already worked one. If He could do one miracle and send him a dog, then God should be able to accomplish *two*.

When the doors of the bus opened, Carter stepped down and looked in both directions. Rusty wasn't there. His heart felt about as heavy as...as a two-ton truck.

"Move," Bailey said, coming down the steps and shoving him in the back.

"Hey," Carter complained.

"You're blocking the exit," Bailey informed him in that prim tattletale voice she sometimes used.

Carter got completely off the bus then and started slowly down the sidewalk to their house. Bailey walked beside him.

"I saw you with that dog on the playground again," his sister said, matching her steps to his. She held her backpack with both hands, leaning into the cold wind.

"You're not gonna tell Mom and Dad, are you?"

"No. He's a nice dog."

Carter nodded. "He's smart, too." But not smart enough to follow bus seven. Not smart enough to know that winter break had begun and there'd be no one at the school to feed him or play with him or anything else. Sooner or later, he'd be picked up by Animal Control.

"You should wash off your coat before Mom sees it," his sister warned.

Carter had forgotten about the mud on his sleeves. "I will. You go in the house first, all right?"

"Okay."

True to her word, Bailey went into the house and while she distracted their mother, Carter removed his coat in their bedroom, then entered the kitchen.

"Ms. Jensen thanked you for the cookies," Carter told his mother. She was folding towels fresh from the dryer on the kitchen table and nodded absently. "Your father's working late this evening," she said. "He's getting overtime pay, and that's good."

"Oh."

"He said we should have dinner without him."

"Can we have macaroni and cheese out of a box?" Carter asked. That was one of his favorites, and he knew it must not cost very much because his mother never objected when he asked for it.

"Okay," she said.

"I wanted hot dogs," Bailey whined.

His mother smiled. "We'll have both."

While his sister helped their mother put away the towels, Carter loped into the bathroom for a clean washcloth and soaked it. Then he wrung it out and took it into the bedroom where he'd put his coat. He wiped off the sleeves. The washcloth got muddy, but his coat looked a lot better.

"Mom said we could watch television," Bailey said, coming into the room.

Since his sister would choose sissy programs, Carter wasn't interested.

"I'm gonna go read."

That was an activity his parents always approved of. The only reason he decided on it now was that he didn't feel like doing anything else. He didn't want to visit his friends or watch television or even play with his toys. He just wanted to forget Rusty. Apparently God only did one miracle at a time. Carter had been wrong.

Slumping down on the floor, he opened his book, but he could hardly concentrate on the story. About fifteen minutes later, his sister barreled into the bedroom. "Carter, come and look!"

"At what?"

"Just come," she insisted, annoying him with every word.

"Oh, all right," he muttered.

She led him to the living room, where the television was situated. She pointed out the front window.

There was Rusty, walking up and down the sidewalk, looking this way and that.

Carter nearly screamed with happiness. "It's Rusty!"

"I know." His sister's eyes were huge.

Without bothering to get his coat, Carter burst out the door. "Rusty!" he cried. "Rusty."

As soon as the dog heard Carter, he turned and bolted toward him. Carter dared not hug him now because his mother would see all the mud. But how could she be angry? God had sent them this dog. Carter had proof that Rusty was the answer to his prayer.

"This way, boy," Carter said and led him to the back of the house. Because their mother had told them their dad would be late, Carter put Rusty in the garage. By the time he'd finished, his teeth were chattering with cold and excitement.

"Are you going to tell Mom?" Bailey asked, meeting him in the hallway.

"Not yet." A plan was taking shape in Carter's mind. "If Mom asks where I am, tell her I'm taking a bath."

"Are you?" Bailey wanted to know.

"No." He shouldn't have to spell *everything* out to his sister. "I'm going to give Rusty one. When he's all cleaned up, Mom will see what a good dog he is and talk Dad into letting me keep him."

Bailey's eyes widened and she nodded conspiratorially.

Carter filled the bathtub with warm water and then at an opportune moment, went into the garage and scooped up Rusty. He was heavier than Carter had thought but it was important that he not leave dog tracks on the floor. Once inside the house, Carter glanced around to make sure his mother wasn't looking. Then he hurried down the hall to the bathroom and shut the door with his foot. He gently set the dog in the bath, then turned quickly to lock the door.

It didn't take Carter long to make a startling discovery about Rusty. When he did, tears sprang to his eyes. Beneath all the caked mud and dirt, Rusty had auburn-colored fur. This really *was* the dog God had sent. He was perfect in every way.

Rusty loved the water. He stood still while Carter lathered him with the shampoo their mother had bought for him and Bailey. Then he rinsed him off with the cup that was by the sink. Rusty didn't bark even once. Using the towel still warm from the dryer, Carter had just lifted Rusty out of the tub to dry him when Rusty began to shake himself like crazy, spraying water in every direction.

"Rusty!" Carter protested, raising his hands to his face to wipe off the water.

"Carter," his mother called from the other side of the bathroom door. "Who's in there with you?"

He wanted to lie and answer *no one,* but he remembered what his stomach had felt like when he'd lied. "A friend," Carter called back. That was true. Rusty was his friend.

"What are you doing in there?"

"Ah…"

The door handle twisted and then his mother called again. "Carter, unlock the door this minute!"

Carter bit his lip as Rusty gazed back at him trustingly. "Okay, boy," he whispered. "It's showtime."

Carter unlatched the bathroom door and opened it for his mother. She stood there, hands on her hips. The moment she saw Rusty, her eyes went soft—and then immediately went hard again.

"Oh, Carter, a dog."

"But this is *my* dog, Rusty. God sent him."

"Carter..." His mother was almost crying. "Look at the bathtub. It's filthy." Sure enough, there was dirt on the bottom of the tub and the ring around the sides was pretty bad, too.

"I'll clean it up," Carter promised. He would've done so earlier, but his mother had interrupted him.

"He's a really good dog, Mom," Carter felt obliged to tell her.

"I'm sure he is, honey. It's just that I don't know what we're going to tell your father."

Carter looked at Rusty and then at the worried expression on his mother's face. He didn't know what they'd tell his dad, either.

12

Harry woke with a start. His eyes flew open as panic overtook him. He gasped for air, unable to get his breath. No matter how hard he struggled, he couldn't breathe. The pain intensified, suffocating him.

Blindly reaching for the small bottle he kept at his bedside, he popped a nitro pill under his tongue and waited. This had happened before in the early hours of the morning. It felt as though he was immersed in water and couldn't get any air.

Could this be his time?

It almost seemed that God intended to take him right then and there. Quelling the panic, Harry surrendered his life to God and then all at once, the ache lessened and his lungs filled with glorious air. The relief was instantaneous. He dragged in a second deep breath and realized he'd had a narrow escape yet again.

Wide awake now, Harry watched the jerky movements of the second hand on the old-fashioned alarm clock by his bedside. Rosalie had a clock radio, but he continued to use the one he'd always had. It needed winding every couple of days, but had served him well through the years and he could see no reason to change. The ticking was a familiar comfort.

Two minutes passed and he was still breathing normally.

His close call reminded him that he wouldn't be around for Rosalie much longer; naturally he wanted to get her settled before he left her. She was determined to spend Christmas in this old house. Harry couldn't deny his wife that. But while he sympathized with her feelings, Harry didn't have that kind of time.

His fear was that when he was gone, Rosalie would just keep putting off the move. Harry couldn't let that happen.

First thing after New Year's, he'd make the arrangements, he decided, praying God would give him that long.

Harry sat up in bed.

"Harry?" Rosalie was instantly awake. The slightest movement on his part seemed to alert her. Similarly, when their girls were small, she'd wakened at the tiniest sound. Harry had never understood it because his wife was usually a sound sleeper. Not when their daughters were young, though, and not with him now.

He'd disturbed her sleep far too many times. After the full day they'd had touring the assisted-living complex Rosalie was exhausted, and Harry didn't want to interrupt her rest tonight.

"I'm fine, sweetheart," he whispered.

Her eyes drifted closed and she went back to sleep. Harry lay very still and listened to the regular cadence of her breathing. Twice his own went shallow and then regained an even consistency.

It went without saying that God had granted him yet another reprieve. Death would come. Not now, but soon—sooner than he would've liked.

When it became apparent that he wasn't going to fall asleep immediately, Harry slowly shifted the covers aside. He might as well empty his bladder, which he needed to do two or three times a night. Darn nuisance it was, but that was another symptom of age and his body's growing demands.

Once he'd finished, he started back to bed and remembered that he'd left his walker in the other room. Since he hated having to use the contraption, he sometimes forgot it. He knew he was in trouble; the short trip to the bathroom had depleted his strength and without the walker, he couldn't manage even the few steps back to his bed. Weak as he was, he leaned his shoulder against the wall, considering his options. There weren't any. He needed help and he needed it now.

"Rosalie," he called. His voice was barely a whisper. As soon as he'd reassured her that he was all right, she'd gone back to sleep. So much for the highly sensitized hearing he'd credited her with a few minutes earlier.

Despite all his resolve, all his determination, Harry began to slide toward the floor. Rosalie wasn't strong enough to help him up. If he fell, he'd stay that way until morning. If he survived until morning....

"Is this it?" Mercy cried, wringing her hands. "Is Harry going to die now?" She needed direction. Her initial response was to hold him upright, to help him. Angels routinely made physical appearances on earth, but it was important to go through the proper channels, to get permission first. She didn't have time for that. She'd certainly bent the rules on occasion, but she couldn't risk interfering with God's plan for Harry.

"Gabriel," she shouted helplessly toward the heavens. "I don't know what to do."

A second later, the archangel was at her side.

"Is it Harry's time to come to heaven?" She pleaded for an answer before daring to take matters into her own hands.

The archangel seemed strangely calm; Mercy was anything but. She hovered close to Harry, anxious to do what she could, awaiting word from Gabriel.

She could tell that Harry's strength was draining away. As she watched, the old man's eyes widened and he placed one hand over his heart.

"Gabriel," Mercy shouted. *"Do something."* Hurriedly she revised her request. "Can I help Harry?" And because she'd come to genuinely love this old man, she added, "Please."

Gabriel nodded. "Take him back to bed."

"Thank you," Mercy whispered, greatly relieved.

Harry's eyes widened again. Only this time it wasn't his heart that worried him. Standing directly in front of him in plain view was a woman dressed in white. A woman with...wings. An angel? She regarded him with a gentle, loving look.

"I could use some help here," he said. In other circumstances Harry might think he'd died. The continuing ache in his chest told him otherwise. The pain intensified with every beat of his heart.

The beautiful angel stepped toward him and silently slipped her arm around his waist. She didn't seem to have any trouble handling his bulk. The next thing

Harry knew, he was in bed and his rescuer was gone. Vanished. She'd disappeared as quickly as she'd come.

Grateful to have averted a catastrophe, or what had seemed like one a few minutes ago, Harry tried to figure out what had just happened. The angel might've been a figment of his imagination except for one thing. He'd been slumped against the wall with no strength left, no ability to stand upright. His walker rested next to his chest of drawers, where it had been all along. But now he was safely tucked into bed, next to Rosalie.

Harry blinked to clear his eyesight and picked up his glasses. Maybe then he'd be able to see the angel a second time. He peered into the darkness, resisting the urge to turn on the light.

She was gone. Truly gone.

Still, Harry was convinced she'd been there. She'd helped him back to bed. What a beauty she'd been, too. He'd always wondered about angels, and now he knew with certainty that they were real.

"Will he be all right now?" Mercy asked, leaning over the slumbering Harry.

"Harry will sleep comfortably for the rest of the night," Gabriel told her.

"In the morning will he remember any of this?" Part of her felt it might be best if the incident was erased from Harry's mind. Then again, she wanted him to know that God was looking down on him, and that he was deeply loved. The mighty angel Gabriel himself had come to Harry's aid.

"He'll remember. This close to death, the separation between heaven and earth is only partially veiled," Gabriel explained.

"It's almost as if Harry has one foot in heaven and one still on earth."

"Exactly." The archangel began to leave, then paused. "I'm proud of you, Mercy," he said.

"You are?" She beamed, but she wasn't sure what she'd done to warrant such high praise. Gabriel didn't issue praise often. He was a strict taskmaster but a fair one.

Apparently reading her mind, Gabriel elaborated. "You didn't take it upon yourself to make a decision on the matter. You turned to heaven and to me for help. That shows a new maturity."

Bubbling with pleasure at his words, Mercy fluttered her wings. Thankfully the archangel hadn't been around when she'd sent Shirley scrambling in the electric cart.

"You did give me cause for concern at the Safeway store, however."

So Gabriel knew.

As if his words had summoned her, Shirley appeared.

"I *knew* Mercy was responsible for that unfortunate event," she cried, glaring at her friend.

"It w-was all in jest," Mercy stammered, embarrassed now. At times, especially while on earth, she adopted a more human nature than an angelic one. As a human might have said, Shirley had been asking for it.

"Shall we discuss this elsewhere?" Gabriel said, gesturing down at the sleeping Harry and Rosalie.

"By all means."

The three of them moved to the living room. When they got there, Mercy saw Goodness on top of the Christmas tree Harry and Rosalie's son-in-law had set up in a corner of the living room.

"Actually, I'm glad to see you, Gabriel," Shirley said. "I'm having the worst time with my assignment."

"Are you, now?" Gabriel asked, eyebrows raised. Mercy and Goodness exchanged a sly glance. They had both agreed that Shirley's was by *far* the least complicated of the assignments.

"It's Carter," Shirley said after a moment's hesitation. "He's found a stray dog."

"And the problem is?"

Shirley shrugged uncomfortably. "The problem is that his father still insists the family can't afford a dog. I was trying to work around that."

"How?" Gabriel asked.

"His father worked overtime this evening and that money will come in handy for Christmas." Shirley rubbed her hands together nervously. "Only..."

"Yes?" Gabriel pressed.

Mercy had to admit she was curious, too, and apparently so was Goodness, because she'd left the Christmas tree to join them.

"Rusty, that's the dog, followed bus number seven home, just like Carter instructed him to."

Gabriel frowned. "Do earthly canines generally understand such detailed instructions?" he asked.

"No," Shirley cried. "That's just the point! I was afraid you'd think I had something to do with it and I promise you I didn't."

"You didn't?" Goodness asked skeptically.

"I'm innocent," Shirley said.

Actually, Mercy would've thought better of her friend if she *had* been involved.

"Every bit of information I've received indicates that Carter is not supposed to have this dog."

"You're sure about that?" Gabriel murmured, and his brow furrowed. "Where's the stray now?"

"This is another problem," Shirley said. "Carter and his mother have put Rusty in the laundry room. Like I told you, David—that's his father—worked late on Friday night and Carter convinced his mother to keep Rusty hidden until morning."

"So the dog's inside the house?"

"For now," Shirley said. "I didn't think Laurie would let him keep the dog for another minute but I was wrong." Shirley shook her head. "I don't know what to tell you about this dog. Not only is he able to read—"

"He *reads?*"

"He knew which bus was number seven, didn't he?"

"Don't you think he might have seen which bus Carter boarded?" Mercy suggested.

"May I please get on with my story?" Shirley asked in dignified tones.

"Don't let me stop you," Mercy muttered. Gabriel sent her a quelling look.

"Not only that, this dog instinctively seems to know who's his friend and who isn't, and he has an uncanny way of making himself scarce when necessary. It's almost as if…as if he has heavenly qualities."

"I find that interesting," Gabriel murmured. "Report back to me on any further developments, will you?"

"Yes, of course."

"Goodness?" Gabriel said, turning to the third angel. "How are you doing?"

"Great! Beth and Peter are about to meet. Isn't it wonderful?"

"Excellent work." And with that, Gabriel returned to heaven.

* * *

Harry woke and saw that Rosalie was awake. "The most astounding thing happened last night," he rushed to tell his wife.

Still sleepy, Rosalie blinked several times. "Did you have another of your attacks?"

"Yes, but that isn't what I want to tell you about."

His wife raised herself up on one elbow. "For heaven's sake, Harry, what's got you so excited?"

"I saw an angel!"

"Now, Harry…"

"I know what you're thinking, Rosalie, but it's true."

His wife frowned, and Harry sensed that she *wanted* to believe what he'd told her but had difficulty accepting it as the truth.

Later that morning, Harry heard his wife chatting on the phone with their youngest daughter. "I'm not sure what to think, Donna. Your father's telling me he saw… Well, he swears he saw an angel."

Harry was sorry now that he'd mentioned this event to Rosalie. She'd apparently concluded that he was losing his mind.

"Yes, yes, I agree," Rosalie said, keeping her voice low. "Please do."

A few minutes later, she hung up and then joined Harry in front of the television. "I was on the phone with Donna," she said conversationally, as if he hadn't noticed. Harry knew exactly who was on the other end of the line.

Nevertheless he didn't comment one way or the other.

"She's going to come early for Christmas. Isn't that nice?"

If the story about the angel had made his youngest daughter decide to come home early, then all the better. His angel had done him even more good than he'd realized.

13

Leavenworth was everything Beth had imagined it would be. When the train pulled in, the sun was shining, and the freshly fallen snow glistened brightly. The entire town was a Christmas wonderland, unlike anything she'd ever seen. Main Street was closed to cars, and in the center of the wide street, burn barrels had been set up, where people could gather to warm their hands. Children were sledding down the short slope next to the gazebo, while a group of costumed carolers entertained the crowd.

It was at this gazebo that Beth Fischer would be meeting Peter in a few hours.

Once they were off the train, Heidi, Sam, two-year-old Adam and Beth toured the area. Adam wanted to go sledding, so Sam quickly purchased a round plastic sled. Soon father and son were gliding down the incline while Heidi took photographs.

"I'll put one of these in our Christmas letter," she told Beth excitedly.

"Isn't it a little late to be mailing out cards?" Beth teased. Heidi was always late. In fact, last year's Christmas cards had arrived in mid-January. Heidi had said that Beth should either consider them very late or exceptionally early.

Beth had been too nervous to eat all day and seeing a vendor selling roasted chestnuts, she purchased a small bag to share with her friend.

Heidi bit into one. "Hey, these aren't bad. They're kind of sweet."

Beth tried one, too, and then another. Now she could say she'd tasted chestnuts roasting on an open fire, just like the Christmas song said.

As they strolled down the street taking in the sights and smells and sounds of Christmas, Beth found herself studying faces. She wondered if Peter's bus had come in yet. Could that tall, handsome man be him? When a little girl leaped into his arms, Beth decided it probably wasn't.

"Are you sorry you agreed to meet Peter so late in the day?"

"Yes," she said tersely.

Soon after that, Sam caught up with them. Adam, bundled from head to foot, was asleep in his father's arms, exhausted from their outing in the snow.

"We were just talking about Beth's appointment," Heidi told her husband.

"I hope you and your WoW partner have a way to connect if something goes wrong," the ever-practical Sam said. "There must be a thousand people here this afternoon."

"Peter e-mailed me his cell phone number."

"Did you give him yours?" Heidi asked.

"No, I didn't think of it." That wasn't completely

accurate. "Actually, I meant to, but we started talking and I forgot."

"That's not a good sign," Sam began. "What if—"

"Sam," Heidi interrupted. "Everything's going to work out fine."

Beth hoped her friend was right. "You'll come with me, won't you?" she asked Heidi. The time was growing closer. At three o'clock, it started to snow. Clouds obscured the sky as dusk fell over the town; by four-thirty it would be completely dark.

"Come with you?" Heidi repeated. "You're kidding, aren't you?"

"Heidi, please. I'm so nervous I'm about to throw up."

"This should be interesting. All you've had to eat is a couple of roasted chestnuts."

"Don't joke," Beth muttered. "I'm serious."

"Okay," Heidi said. "I'll come if you really want me to, but I'm only going to stay long enough for the two of you to meet."

"What if we don't like each other?" Beth asked, feeling a sense of dread. She was bringing so many hopes, so much yearning, to this encounter that she was afraid she'd set herself up for failure.

The night before, as they exchanged instant messages, Peter was the one who'd seemed anxious.

They'd tried to reassure each other. That was when he'd given her his phone number. Online they had so much to talk about, and Beth sincerely hoped the chemistry that seemed to spark between them on the screen translated into real life.

At ten minutes to four, Beth and Heidi made their way toward the gazebo, where Peter would be waiting for her. She'd know him by the long-stemmed red rose and his Seahawks hat.

"This is the most romantic date I've ever heard about," Heidi said dreamily.

Beth slipped her arm through Heidi's. "I'm so grateful you're here."

They stood in the background because Beth was feeling shy and a bit shaky, which could've been low blood sugar, Heidi told her. In any event, her plan was to wait for him and then casually walk up and introduce herself.

"There he is!" Heidi said, pointing toward a cluster of people near the gazebo.

"Where? Where? I don't see him." And then she did.

"Beth, oh my goodness, look at him! He's *gorgeous*."

Beth froze and her heart sank to her knees. Her stomach pitched wildly. "He's that, all right," she whispered numbly.

"How did you get so lucky?" Heidi was too excited to notice Beth's complete lack of enthusiasm.

"I don't know," Beth said, her voice low and emotionless.

Heidi turned to stare at her. "What's the matter with you? Peter looks like he stepped off the pages of a romance novel."

"He does, doesn't he?" Beth murmured. Then she covered her face with both hands and turned away. Whipping the red hat off her head, she quickly unwrapped the telltale scarf from around her neck, as well.

"Beth, what's wrong?" Heidi asked.

"What's wrong?" Beth repeated. "You want me to tell you what's wrong? That Peter is an imposter!"

"How can he be an imposter when you've never met him before?"

"His name isn't Peter," she choked out. "It's John Nicodemus and he's my ex-husband."

That news seemed to shock her friend. *"What?"*

"Let's get out of here before he sees me," Beth urged. Heidi couldn't possibly have known what John looked like, because she and Heidi hadn't met until five years ago—and she certainly didn't keep wedding photos at her desk or in her condo.

Together they hurried around the corner and Beth flattened herself against the side of a building.

"What are you going to do?" Heidi asked curiously.

Beth needed to think. At first she'd been numb with shock, but now she was angry. "He planned this. He knew all along."

"Beth, that's not fair. How could he have?"

"We never exchanged last names. And he changed his first name, didn't he? He tricked me."

Heidi shook her head. "Didn't you tell me you shortened your name to Beth after your divorce?"

"I did," she admitted. "I wanted to make a fresh start, so I decided that from then on, I'd just use Beth."

"Perhaps John did the same thing," Heidi suggested.

Beth wasn't willing to concede the point. "His middle name is Peter," she said grudgingly. "It never occured to me..."

"He *is* gorgeous, though."

"His good looks are the only thing he has going for him," Beth mumbled.

"That isn't what you told me earlier."

"What do you mean?" Heidi wasn't usually this argumentative. Clearly, she was taking Peter/John's side, and that infuriated Beth.

"Don't you remember what you said last week?" Heidi asked. "You told me Peter is everything your first husband wasn't."

"I said that?" What an idiot she'd been. What an imbecile. She'd allowed John to make a fool of her. He knew who she was. He *had* to have known. How could he not? But maybe...just maybe, he didn't. Could they have found each other online? No one would believe something this random could actually happen. It was more than bizarre. It was completely and totally im-plausible…wasn't it?

"You can't leave him standing there waiting for you like that," Heidi insisted. "That would be cruel."

Beth didn't respond, still trying to figure out how this had happened. It dawned on her that he *couldn't* have known, since he'd been the one to suggest she meet him outside the gazebo. If he'd known, he would never have given her the opportunity to see him first and then walk away. Unlikely though it seemed, she had to conclude that he was as much in the dark as she was.

"Did you hear me?" Heidi demanded. "You have to call him on his cell."

"No, you have to," Beth said frantically.

"I beg your pardon?" Heidi looked confused.

"Use my phone." She thrust it at her friend.

"Why me? Beth, you're the one who should talk to him, not me." She refused to accept the phone.

"I can't… He'll recognize my voice." He would, too. It might've been almost ten years since the di-vorce, but that wouldn't matter. John would know her voice the same way she would his.

"You don't want him to find out it's you?" Heidi asked, sounding even more confused.

"No. Not yet. I need to think." This awkward situation had to be handled delicately or John might assume she'd tricked him—which was what *she'd* suspected about him.

"Here—I'll do it," Heidi said and snatched the phone away from her. "What should I tell him?"

Beth hadn't thought that far ahead. "I—I'm not sure."

"Should I say something came up at the last minute and you had to leave?"

"But if he asks what it is…" Beth was growing desperate.

"He won't," Heidi said. "Anyway, something did come up, so it isn't like you're lying."

Beth shrugged helplessly.

"Give me his cell phone number." Heidi held out her hand.

Digging through her purse, Beth nearly dumped the entire contents in the snow.

"Relax," Heidi said in an annoyingly calm voice. "Re-e-lax."

Beth scowled at her, and as soon as she found the crumpled slip of paper with his phone number, she slapped it in Heidi's hand.

Heidi punched out the number, holding the phone close to Beth's ear.

Peter/John answered on the first ring. "Hello."

"Is this Peter?"

"Beth? Where are you?"

Heidi glanced at Beth, who gestured for her to continue speaking. "I'm so sorry, Peter, but I can't make it. Something, uh, came up—at the last minute and I can't keep our appointment. I'm *so* disappointed." This last part was said with feeling.

"I am, too," Peter responded. "I didn't know what to think when you didn't show up at four."

"I'd like to meet you. I really would—just not now. Can we arrange another time?"

Beth glared at her friend. She made a frenzied cutting motion with one hand but Heidi ignored her, turning her back on Beth.

Beth hurried around in order to face her. Once

more, she made exaggerated cutting motions, using both hands to emphasize the point.

"Next Friday, after Christmas, would be perfect," Heidi went on to say. "Since I was the one who let you down, please come to my place. Yes, yes, I'm sure."

Beth's mouth fell open. Her friend had really crossed the line with that one. Before she could stop her, Heidi rattled off Beth's address.

A moment later, Heidi clicked the cell phone shut and returned it to Beth.

"Have you gone insane?" Beth cried. "You gave him my address!"

"Well, yes, that's what you wanted me to do, isn't it?"

"No…yes. Oh, I don't know." Beth's ears felt frozen and she covered them with her hands. She didn't dare put on her hat until they were far from the gazebo.

"That gives you six days to prepare him."

"You're worried about *John?*" Some friend Heidi had turned out to be!

"Not John," Heidi explained patiently. "I'm concerned about Peter, the man you fell in love with over the last six months."

Then it hit Beth, something she'd completely forgotten. "He's married."

"What do you mean, he's married?"

"A friend told me she'd heard John remarried and if that's the case, he's either divorced a second time or cheating on his wife." A sick feeling attacked her stomach.

"My guess is that your friend was talking about some other John."

"It can't be…" Or could it? Beth no longer knew. All she did know was that she had six days to sort this out before she confronted Peter/John with the truth.

14

Early Saturday morning, Carter tiptoed down to the laundry room as quietly as he could. After working late at the pizza place he managed, his father hadn't come home until way past Carter's bedtime. Carter had lain awake, worrying that his father would somehow discover Rusty in the house. If he did, he just might take the dog away in the middle of the night.

When Carter heard the garage door close, he'd prayed really hard that Rusty wouldn't bark at the strange noise. The dog seemed to have a sixth sense about things like that, because he stayed quiet all night.

Carter could hear his parents talking, and even though he'd had his ear against the door, he couldn't make out their words. All he knew was that after about ten minutes they went to bed. Then and only then was Carter able to sleep.

In the morning, he sneaked down the hallway and freed Rusty from the laundry room. Rusty wanted outside, and Carter let him into the backyard to do his business. As soon as he'd finished, Rusty hurried back onto the porch, where Carter waited for him.

"Are you hungry, boy?" Carter asked softly. No one else in the house was awake. He bent down and stroked the rich auburn fur of his new best friend. Then he led Rusty back into the laundry room and filled his water dish. He gave him a bowl of Wheaties with milk because they didn't have any dog food.

Rusty seemed to like the cereal and when he'd licked the bowl clean, Carter returned to his bedroom. The dog walked politely beside him. Without being asked, Carter made his bed, dressed and brushed his teeth, too. All the while, Rusty lay on his bedroom rug, his eyes never leaving Carter.

When he heard his parents stir, Carter was ready. He knew it would take a lot of fast talking to convince his father to let him keep Rusty. His one hope was that once he heard Rusty had followed him home, he'd understand that this was a special dog. This was the dog God had sent Carter.

Through his partially open door, he could hear his father step into the kitchen and immediately start making coffee. Rusty dashed out of the bedroom before Carter could stop him. He raced after the dog but it was too late. Rusty skidded into the kitchen, his long tail wagging excitedly.

His father caught sight of Rusty and bent down to pet him. "Where did you come from, boy?" he asked.

"Hi, Dad," Carter said tentatively.

"Do you have a friend spending the night?" David asked, glancing at his son.

Carter swallowed hard. "Rusty's my friend."

"Rusty?" his father repeated.

"I named him after the dog you had when you were a kid. You told me about him, remember?"

Slowly his father nodded. "Where did you get the dog, Carter?"

Carter's mother came into the kitchen just then, tying the sash on her housecoat. She looked uneasily from Carter to his father. "I meant to tell you about Rusty last night, David," she said, pouring them each a cup of coffee.

"I suppose it slipped your mind," David commented, frowning.

"No. I decided you were too tired and didn't need to deal with another problem. We couldn't do anything until morning anyway."

His father turned to Carter. "Where did you get the dog?" he asked a second time.

"He was in the schoolyard, but Dad, this is a *special* dog. Really special. Out of all the kids there, Rusty came to me."

"Did you feed him?"

"He was starving, Dad! And his coat was all muddy and…he needs a family."

"You gave him something to eat, didn't you?"

"Yes." Carter bit his lip. "I fed him a Twinkie and then Bailey let me have her peanut-butter-and-jelly sandwich." Because he wanted his father to know his sister hadn't willingly donated her sandwich, he explained. "I traded my Saturday TV privileges, though, so Bailey would give me her sandwich."

"Carter," his father said gently. "Rusty came to you because he thought you'd feed him."

"Not at first," Carter insisted. "He didn't know about the Twinkie."

"He could probably smell it in your pocket. Dogs have a keen sense of smell."

"Oh."

"As for him following you home?"

"Yes, he...Rusty's not just any dog. He's smart and he listens and he understands, too."

His father crouched down so they were eye to eye. "Did you encourage him to follow you?" he asked.

"He followed the bus! I told you, Dad—he's smart."

Reaching out, his father rested a hand on Carter's shoulder. "Rusty could see that you liked him."

"It's more than that!" Carter cried. "I prayed really hard and God sent me Rusty. He was so muddy I...I didn't even know his fur was red until I gave him a bath."

"In our tub?" his father asked.

Carter nodded reluctantly.

His father stood and cast him a disapproving look.

"Did he make a mess?" The question was directed at Carter's mother.

"I cleaned it up," Carter inserted. "Tell him, Mom, tell Dad that I washed out the bathtub and everything."

"He did," she confirmed, handing his father a mug of fresh coffee.

David accepted it, closing his eyes as he took his first sip. "I'm glad you cleaned up after the dog."

Relieved, Carter offered his father a hopeful smile. "It was like God was telling me this dog was for me because he had red fur."

A pained look appeared on his father's face. "Did you stop to think that Rusty might belong to another little boy?"

The thought had never entered Carter's mind. "Rusty might have another family?"

His father set the mug aside and put his hand on Carter's shoulder once again. "There could be a little boy out there who's lost his dog."

"Not Rusty," Carter said with certainty.

"We can't be sure of anything when it comes to a stray."

Carter shook his head. "Rusty needs a family," he stated boldly. "*Our* family. He adopted us."

The same sad look came over his father. "I wish we could keep him. He seems like a nice dog."

"He's a *wonderful* dog, and he's housebroken and he doesn't eat much. He can have my food."

David drew one hand across his face. "If it was just a matter of food, we could deal with that, but it isn't. I already explained this to you, Carter. There are the vet's fees for one thing. Since Rusty's been on the streets for a while, he should be checked out by a veterinarian."

"I'll pay for it with my allowance," Carter said. "I have thirty dollars and seventy-six cents."

"David," his mother murmured in a soft, pleading voice.

"That wouldn't begin to cover the cost of a checkup and shots. And what if he needs some kind of treatment? Then there's the license and heaven knows what else. We can't keep him, Carter. I don't want to sound heartless but we'd be doing Rusty a disservice, too."

Carter didn't want to cry but his eyes filled with tears before he could hold them back.

His mother wrapped her arms around him and held him close. "I'm so sorry, honey," she whispered.

"Where will you take him?" Carter sobbed, looking up at his father.

"He'll have to go to the animal shelter."

"No, Daddy, *please!*" Bailey came into the kitchen, dragging her stuffed Winnie the Pooh bear on the linoleum. She was still in her pajamas and her hair was all frizzy because she'd gone to bed with it wet.

"Can't Rusty stay until Christmas?" Carter begged.

"That'll just make it harder to give him up," his father said. "Besides, we don't know if he's picked up any parasites, and the sooner he's checked out, the better."

Rusty lay down on the small rug in front of the

kitchen sink and rested his head on his paws. Bailey sat on the floor next to him.

"Get up, Bailey. He probably has fleas."

"No, he doesn't, Dad," Carter said. "I washed him real good. Ask Mom."

"We'll take him down to the shelter this afternoon," his father said, not waiting to see if Bailey obeyed him. He walked out of the kitchen.

"Mom?" Carter could feel the tears running down his face.

"You heard your father." She looked like she wanted to cry, too.

"But…"

"Remember what Dad said about some other little boy losing Rusty? Can you imagine how happy he'll be to find him?"

Carter tried to imagine what it would be like to lose his dog and how awful he'd feel. Sniffling, he wiped his cheeks with one sleeve.

"If we take Rusty to the animal shelter, that little boy will get him back," his mother went on in a reassuring voice.

Being brave was hard, but Carter did his best. His lower lip quivered and he sat down on the floor and buried his face in the dog's fur. Bailey sat on Rusty's other side, clutching her bear and murmuring sweetly. As if seeking a way to comfort him, Rusty licked Carter's hand.

"You might have another family that loves you even more than I do." Carter's voice broke as he spoke to the dog.

"Carter," his mother said softly. "As soon as we can afford it, you'll have your dog. I talked to Mrs. Smith at the school, and she said there'll be an opening at the cafeteria in February. I'm going to apply for it and if I get the job, then you can have a dog."

Hope flared and then just as quickly died. "But it won't be Rusty."

"No," his mother agreed, "it won't be Rusty."

"I don't want any dog except Rusty."

"Oh, Carter."

"I mean it, Mom. Rusty's the only dog I want."

"I should never have let you bring him in the house," his mother said, and she sounded angry with herself.

"It just makes this more difficult. I'm so sorry, honey, but your dad's right. We can't give Rusty the kind of home he needs."

"Rusty is Carter's dog," Bailey wailed. She held her Pooh bear tight against her chest, as if she was afraid their father would take her stuffed friend to the animal shelter, too.

"Can I call Grandma?" Carter asked. His grandparents were his last hope. If he explained everything to them, maybe they'd be willing to pay for the checkup, the dog license and whatever else Rusty needed.

"Your grandparents are gone this weekend," his mother said.

"I can't call them?"

"No, Carter, they're visiting friends in Seattle."

"Oh."

Carter knew he didn't have any choice. He had to give up his dog. He spent all morning with Rusty, talking to him. Bailey used her own hairbrush to comb the dog's fur until it was shiny and bright. Rusty stood still and even seemed to enjoy Bailey's ministrations.

Midafternoon, his father came into Carter and Bailey's bedroom. "You ready, son?" he asked.

Carter wouldn't ever be ready. He hugged Rusty around the neck, face buried in his fur, and nodded.

"You don't have to come with me."

"I want to," Carter said stubbornly.

His father sighed. "Okay, then. Let's go."

Rusty seemed to think they were going to a fun place, because the instant David opened the car door, he leaped inside and lay down in the backseat next to Carter.

His father didn't say a single word on the ride to the shelter in Wenatchee.

Neither did Carter. He stroked Rusty's head and struggled not to cry.

The county animal shelter was busy. Lots of people had come by to choose dogs and cats during the Christmas holidays. Some other family would be getting Rusty. Some other little boy would get Carter's special dog.

"You can stay in the car if you want," his father told him.

"No." Carter was determined to be with his dog as long as he possibly could.

His father went inside the shelter and came back with a woman who was carrying a collar and leash. Carter listened as his father spoke to the lady.

"My son found Rusty in the schoolyard, and the dog followed him home. According to my wife, the poor thing was caked in mud. He seems to be a gentle dog, and he's obviously had some training, so I assume he's lost."

His father opened the passenger door and Rusty raised his head expectantly.

The woman reached into the car and stroked Rusty's head. "Oh, what an attractive dog he is. Probably part Irish setter—they're a nice breed. We could've adopted him out a dozen times over earlier in the day."

This wasn't news Carter wanted to hear. "What about his other family? My dad said there might be other people who owned Rusty." That was his one comfort—that bringing Rusty to the shelter might help the dog locate his original owner.

The lady from the shelter sighed. "His other family didn't take very good care of him, though, did they?" she said. "Rusty didn't have any identification on him, did he?"

"No," Carter admitted.

She examined the insides of Rusty's ears. "No tattoos, either."

"How will you figure out who owns him, then?" Carter asked.

"We can check for a microchip, but I doubt we'll find one. Without that, there's no way of knowing where his family is," she explained. "Still, this is the best time of year to guarantee him a good home. I'm sure he'll be adopted quickly. That's what you want for him, isn't it?" She looked directly at Carter.

Hard though it was to agree, Carter nodded. With his heart breaking, he threw his arms around Rusty for one last hug.

15

All day Rosalie had been fluttering about the house, getting ready for their daughters' arrival. Harry was exhausted by all the activity around him. She'd changed the sheets on the beds and while he wanted to help her with the guest room, he couldn't. Without his saying a word, his wife seemed to realize how much he hated his physical limitations. Twice she made a special trip into the family room, where Harry sat watching television, to give him a kiss on the forehead.

"Donna will get here tomorrow afternoon," Rosalie announced for about the tenth time that morning. "Donna and Richard are coming first, and Lorraine and Kenny will drive over on Christmas Eve. The grandkids are coming then, too. Did I tell you that already?"

He nodded. Her memory wasn't the problem in this instance; Rosalie was just plain excited. Chattering incessantly was something Rosalie did when she was happy. And although Harry wasn't constantly talking about his daughters' visit, he felt the same joy. It'd been a lot of years since their two girls had spent Christmas with them. The whole family would be together. According to Dr. Snellgrove, this would be his last Christmas on earth, and for Rosalie's sake, he wanted it to be a good one; having their daughters with them would ensure that.

"The girls don't want you to worry about cooking," Harry reminded his wife. There'd been two or three conversations that very day between his daughters and Rosalie. Lorraine had insisted on ordering a special ham for their Christmas dinner and would be bringing it with her. Donna had a scalloped potato recipe she planned to make. As for the other side dishes, apparently their daughters were taking care of those, as well. And Rosalie was baking the family's favorite pie for Christmas Day dessert.

Although the menu had long been determined, his wife spent hours poring over cookbooks. Harry didn't know why. But seeing her this involved raised his own spirits.

She hadn't mentioned the appearance of the angel. Not since he'd told her about it. Afterward, Harry had done quite a bit of thinking. That angel had been real. As real as Rosalie. Most important, she'd been there, at his side. Harry would never have made it back to bed without her.

That led him to remember again what the young doctor had told him. Anytime, Dr. Snellgrove had said. Death was getting close. Harry could feel it. Every day he seemed to grow weaker. Every day it became more difficult to accomplish even the simplest and most mundane tasks, such as dressing and shaving. When he'd finished brushing his teeth, he was nearly too weak to stand.

"I thought I'd bake cinnamon rolls for breakfast

Christmas morning," Rosalie was saying as she stalked through the family room, a feather duster in one hand. She swiped the thing every which way, swirling up dust left and right.

"Rosalie," Harry protested.

"Sorry, sweetheart, but I want the house to look its best for the girls."

In a blur, his wife dashed past him and into the next room. Where she found the energy, Harry couldn't even imagine. Next he caught sight of her fluffing up the sofa pillow, squeezing it hard, then pounding it into place. Harry couldn't help smiling.

"Rosalie," he called out. "Sit down a minute, would you? I'm getting tired just watching you."

"I don't have time to sit."

"I need to talk to you."

"All right, all right." The way she breezed into the room reminded him of Loretta Young's entrance on her television show in the fifties. He'd seen that moment hundreds of times, and it lingered in his mind to this day. Rosalie had been every bit as beautiful as Loretta Young back then. Still was, in his opinion.

"Sit." Harry pointed to her chair, which stood next to his own. They shared an end table and a lamp.

"Yes, sweetheart?" She sat on the very edge of her seat, signaling her impatience to get on with her work.

"I was thinking we should talk about Liberty Orchard."

"Harry Alderwood, I told you—I don't have time to talk about this now."

"Please?" he asked quietly. It had been weighing on him all day.

Rosalie released a gusty sigh that the neighbors could probably have heard if they'd been listening. "*Must* we?"

"It would put my mind at rest," he told her.

She sighed again, accepting that he wasn't going to let this drop. "Fine. If you feel it's that important, then let's talk."

Harry was grateful. If possible, he'd like Rosalie's future settled before the girls arrived. He knew it was necessary to set things in motion, which meant they had to secure the unit. Harry felt an urgency that his recent heavenly visitation had only heightened. He might have mere days to live. Mere days to arrange all of this.

"You said you didn't want to think about moving until after the holidays," he began, "but—"

"I don't," Rosalie broke in. "I've got enough to do with the girls and their husbands coming here for Christmas."

"I agree."

She seemed surprised by that.

"But," he added before she could crow at her apparent victory, "I'd be more comfortable if we told the administrator we've decided to take the unit."

Rosalie hesitated. "Do you really think a few more days will make that much difference?"

"Yes," Harry said firmly. "It'd give me peace of mind."

Rosalie folded her hands in her lap. "I don't know, Harry..."

"What's to know?" Dear heaven, Rosalie couldn't have changed her mind already, could she?

"Harry, we've been in this house for so many years. To give it up like this... I don't think I'm ready."

"You said—"

She held up her hand. "I *know* what I said. Yes, we had a good time at Liberty Orchard. Lucy's always been a persuasive person. And at first I was excited to see my friends again, but now..." She let the words fade and refused to meet his eyes.

"But now?" Harry prodded.

"Now I'm not sure we should be in such a rush. Let's talk to the girls about it some more."

"They'll agree with me."

"I agree with you, too, Harry. But why do we have to do it right this minute? It's going to be hard on me to leave this house, you know."

"I know. For me, too." It would be even harder for him to leave Rosalie and his family.

"I'm going to call the administrator," he said.

"Harry!" Rosalie gasped.

"If we change our minds, we'll only be out a few hundred dollars." Despite what Rosalie thought, Harry was convinced Mrs. Goldsmith hadn't been lying. He believed someone else *was* interested in that unit. So he wanted to make the deposit immediately.

"A few hundred dollars?" Rosalie repeated in a

stunned voice. "Since when have we ever had money to burn, Harry Alderwood?"

As children of the Depression, Harry and Rosalie had lived frugally. They'd budgeted their entire lives and saved ten percent of every dollar earned. Neither one wasted anything. Rosalie even kept those plastic bags from the grocery store. Young people these days didn't know the value of a dollar. And credit cards! He'd seen more people get into financial trouble because of those cards.

"This will be money well invested," Harry assured his wife.

Rosalie continued to look uncertain. "If you're positive this is what you want—"

"It is," Harry said, cutting her off. "You know, Rosalie, that angel was real."

She frowned.

"I needed help. I collapsed and I couldn't get up. I wouldn't have managed without her."

Her frown deepened. "You're on a lot of medication."

He realized this was the rationale Donna must have offered her mother when he'd heard the two of them discussing the incident. In fact, that conversation was what had prompted his youngest daughter to visit a day early. "All I know is that I was in trouble and I didn't have my walker and then...I was back in bed."

"Why didn't you call me? If you needed help, I would've come right away."

"I would have if I'd had the strength." As he recalled, Harry had made an effort to rouse his wife, to no avail. Not that she could've helped him up or supported him on the walk into the bedroom.

Rosalie got to her feet. "I can see you're determined, so go ahead and make that phone call," she said. "We'll both adjust. You're right, Harry. If it was up to me, I'd put off the move indefinitely. We need to start making plans."

Relief washed over him. As soon as his wife went back to her fussing and cleaning, Harry removed his wallet from his hip pocket—a procedure that left him short of breath—and took out the business card the administrator had given him.

Elizabeth Goldsmith.

He reached for the portable phone. They had three phones in the house, thanks to Lorraine. One in the bedroom, another in the kitchen and the third next to his recliner on the small end table.

Although it was a Saturday, the administrator had promised him she'd be available.

A woman with a pleasant voice answered the phone. "Liberty Orchard," she said brightly. "How might I direct your call?"

"I'd like to speak with Elizabeth Goldsmith."

"One moment, please."

"Thank you." Harry closed his eyes, afraid that if Rosalie looked his way, she might try to talk him into waiting, despite the fact that he'd made the best decision. The only decision.

"Elizabeth Goldsmith," he heard half a minute later.

"Harry Alderwood," he returned. He didn't understand why people felt they had to announce their names when they answered the phone. He knew whom he'd called and presumably Elizabeth knew who she was. He'd noticed that it had become a common business practice in the last few years.

"Ah, yes, we spoke recently, didn't we?" Elizabeth said.

"My wife, Rosalie, and I were by to see the facility a few days ago."

"Ah, yes. You're friends of Lucy Menard's, aren't you?"

"Yes."

Harry got right to the point. "When we spoke, you confirmed that you had one unit open."

"Yes." Elizabeth paused. "But—"

He continued to speak, eager to get this done. "We discussed my giving you a check to secure that unit," he said.

"Yes, I do recall that I urged you to make the deposit right away."

He was well aware of that and had thought of little else since their meeting.

"I mentioned that there was only one unit open, didn't I?" she went on.

"Yes." Harry was beginning to worry just a bit.

"And I did mention that someone else had shown an interest?"

"Yes, you did."

"Well, I'm afraid, Mr. Alderwood, that the first party came back the following day with a check."

"You mean…the unit's already been taken?" He could hear the stunned disbelief in his own voice.

"I'm afraid so. And unfortunately there was only the one."

He wished she'd quit reminding him of that.

"How soon will you have another unit available?" Harry asked, still in shock.

Elizabeth considered her answer. "That's difficult to say. It could be three months but it might be as long as six."

"Oh."

"I'm sorry, Mr. Alderwood."

"No…no, I'm the one who's sorry. You suggested we decide quickly and I thought we had."

"If there's anything else I can do for you, please let me know. Oh, and in the meantime, Merry Christmas."

"Thank you. Merry Christmas to you." He put back the phone and released a deep sigh of regret, knowing he should have taken action that very day.

Now it was too late.

Too late for him.

In three months' time he wouldn't be here. In three months' time Rosalie would be a widow.

16

Beth slept fitfully all night. She couldn't escape the thoughts tumbling crazily through her mind, but every once in a while exhaustion overtook her, and she'd slip into a light sleep. Then she'd dream—dreams filled with John. And the shock of what she'd discovered would jerk her awake. Before long, the whole process would start all over again.

In the morning, she was blurry-eyed and her temples were throbbing with the beginnings of a headache. Despite how she felt, she had no choice but to attend Mass. James and Bella, her nephew and niece, were participating in a special Christmas program. Not to show up would disappoint them. Besides, her entire family would be there; it was easier to make the effort and go now than to offer excuses later.

Before she left, Beth swallowed two aspirin with a glass of orange juice. Her mother had planned a large brunch afterward.

By the time Beth arrived at the church, the parking lot was almost full. She hoped her mother had saved her a place.

Joyce was lying in wait just inside the church vestibule, which meant she had something on her mind—and Beth could easily guess what it was.

"You're late and it's time for Mass," her mother said, slipping her arm around Beth, as if she was afraid her daughter might make a run for it at the last minute. "Your father saved us two places, but I don't think he'll be able to hold on to them much longer."

"Sorry, Mom, I got a slow start."

"I want to hear every detail about Leavenworth."

Joyce narrowed her eyes. "*Every* detail," she repeated ominously.

"Yes, well… I'll explain later." She wouldn't tell her family everything, though. She felt overwhelmed by the events of the day before. Heidi's arrangement with Peter—John—on her behalf was a further complication, one she didn't need. But the immediate problem was how much to say to her parents.

As soon as Mass began, Beth's problems seemed to lift from her shoulders. The beauty of the church, with its decorations of poinsettia and evergreen boughs, the joyful music and the sermon's message—about forgiving yourself and not allowing past mistakes to hold you back—seemed to be just for her. The Christmas pageant was delightful and when she joined in the carol-singing, her heart felt free.

That morning, her entire life had felt like a disaster. By the end of Mass, Beth had begun to feel a new sense of hope. Maybe this bizarre coincidence involving John was meant to be. Maybe…maybe they'd have a second chance, despite all the bitterness and grief.

The family brunch at her parents' home was her only remaining hurdle today. Everyone wanted to know about Peter.

"Don't keep us in suspense," her mother said as she passed the platter of scrambled eggs to Beth.

"Mom, please." Foolishly she'd hoped to avoid lengthy explanations and at first she'd thought that might actually happen, since everyone's attention was focused on her niece and nephew, who'd played minor roles in today's program. But she should've known it wouldn't be that easy. At Joyce's comment, everyone stopped eating and stared at Beth.

"We're just curious," her sister added. "If you tell us to mind our own business, we will."

"Angela," their mother said. "Don't even suggest Marybeth keep this to herself!"

Groaning, Beth could see that it was useless to resist. Her mother felt entitled to an answer—and it had better be the right answer, too. Joyce had lit a candle, after all.

"Yesterday I—" Beth thought about telling the truth. The direct approach had its benefits. But the thought of explaining that Peter wasn't Peter but John Nicodemus, her ex-husband, was more than she could handle. As her mental debate continued, Beth hesitated, leaving her sentence unfinished.

"Marybeth, *please,*" her mother implored.

"We didn't meet," she blurted out.

"You didn't meet?" The question echoed around the table.

"Don't tell me you chickened out," her mother cried. The horrified look was back, as if Beth had, once again, been a disappointment to the family.

She couldn't tell them the real reason she hadn't met Peter, so she just sat and gazed blankly at the wall.

After a moment, her parents' eyes met. Her father cleared his throat. "Actually, your mother and I suspected this might happen. We feel it's time, Beth, for you to consider counseling."

"What?" Beth couldn't believe what she was hearing.

"Your father and I are willing to pay for it," her mother put in.

There was no point in arguing. Beth could see they weren't going to budge from their decision. "I don't object to counseling," she murmured. "In theory, that is. I just don't think I need it."

"You need it," her mother said grimly.

"Can we talk about this after Christmas?" Beth asked, wanting to delay any further discussion until she'd had time to analyze her own reactions to the Peter/John confusion.

"Of course we can," her sister assured her sympathetically.

So her sister was in on this, as well. That loving, compassionate look was a dead giveaway.

Beth left her parents' home shortly after the brunch dishes had been washed and put away. As she drove back to her own place, she deliberated on what to say to Peter. Despite the fact that he was really John, she'd come to think of him as Peter—a new man. A *different* man.

Once home, she shed her coat and purse and logged on to the Internet. The moment she did, Peter sent her an instant message.

I wondered when you'd get here.

His comment indicated that he'd been waiting for her to come online.

I'm here now, she typed back. **I want to talk to you about meeting later this week.**

Are you having second thoughts?

She mulled over her answer. **Yes. You see, I've already made one disastrous mistake in my life when it comes to relationships and I'm not eager to make another.**

In other words, you're gun-shy.

Frankly, yes.

This might surprise you, Peter wrote back, **but I am, too.**

Really? Then because she couldn't resist, she asked, **Was your marriage that horrible?**

I guess not. We were both young and immature.

Beth couldn't leave it at that. This was a perfect opportunity to discover exactly what Peter thought of her. **Do you have any regrets?**

He didn't reply right away. **Some.**

Me, too, she told him. **More than I realized.**

Has your ex remarried? Peter typed.

This was a tricky question. **I heard he did.**

So you don't keep tabs on him?

No. What about your ex-wife?

I have no idea. We went our separate ways. I don't harbor any ill will toward her. I couldn't tell you if she's remarried or not.

Did you love her? For one long heartbeat, Beth's finger was poised above the key that would submit her question. Her mind raced; she was afraid this was one she shouldn't be asking. She sent it anyway.

His answer came in the form of another question. Did you love your ex?

Her reply was simple. Yes. I guess I still do in some ways. And you?

Yes. A short pause and then he added, Is that the real problem? Are you so in love with your ex that you aren't ready to fall in love a second time?

Peter deserved the truth—but not yet. He admitted he'd loved her once, maybe still did, but preferred not to discuss her.

What Peter couldn't know was that she had information he didn't....

Listen, let's put the matter of our former marriages to rest. His next words flashed across the screen. My wife and I behaved badly. We were both at fault and I've accepted that our problems were complex. I've moved on and apparently so has she. Although painful, the divorce was for the best.

The best? Beth read those words and her throat tightened.

I wish her well and I'm sure you don't begrudge your ex-husband happiness. Am I right?

Yes, she typed back.

Good. Then let's drop the subject. Agreed?

Beth read his words, then pressed her fingers to her lips as she wondered how to respond. Agreed...only I'm not sure the timing is right for the two of us.

In what way?

It's Christmas, and I have enough family pressures without worrying about what will happen once we meet.

I know what you mean.

Shall we put this off? she asked.

For how long?

Why don't we wait until after New Year's.

Okay.

His clipped reply implied that he was disappointed. Well, she was, too, but she couldn't spring the news on Peter like this, two days before the biggest holiday of the year.

You aren't going to duck out on me again, are you? Peter asked.

Beth appreciated his directness. **No,** she typed. **I'd just like a little more time.**

Whatever you say. But I believe it's important for both of us to put the past behind us.

"Behind us," Beth repeated aloud. Little did Peter know how impossible that would be.

"After New Year's?" Goodness gasped, leaning over Beth's shoulder to read her messages.

"What's wrong?" Mercy asked.

As far as Goodness was concerned, *everything* was wrong. Nothing was going the way she'd planned. She'd worked so hard, too, trying to bring these two lonely humans together.

"They *have* to meet before Christmas Eve," she muttered.

Mercy nodded. "So what are you going to do about it?"

Goodness smiled; a plan was already taking shape in her mind. She didn't want to intervene in human events; strictly speaking, that was against the rules. However, Beth and Peter weren't giving her much of an alternative. Either she acted on their behalf or Gabriel would have to report that she'd failed. No one would blame her for a small intervention, least of all Gabriel, but so far her track record had been exceptional—if she did say so herself—and she wanted to keep it that way.

Everyone in heaven knew that humans were difficult subjects. At times they required a clear and unambiguous sign, or a bit of coaxing. Or both. And some people needed more help than others. In Goodness's opinion, Beth was one of those.

"Well, you have to admit we all had a shock," Mercy said, reminding Goodness of the scene in Leavenworth the day before.

"I agree." Goodness frowned as she contemplated her next move. Letting Peter and Beth stumble into each other on the street would be too convenient—and too subtle. No, whatever Goodness arranged would have to be dramatic. Personally she'd prefer a car crash, involving a massive explosion—no deaths, of course. The possibility of a SWAT team thrilled her and if she could manage it, a helicopter rescue. That would make her day. Those boys in black always did get her adrenaline going.

"Goodness," Mercy prodded gently. "I recognize that look in your eyes and I don't like the way your wings are fluttering."

"I think it might be best if you left now," she said primly.

"Goodness!"

"I don't want you to get in trouble, too."

Mercy's wings lifted her off the ground. "*What* are you going to do?"

Goodness pressed her lips together and shook her head. "It's better for you not to know."

That was when Shirley arrived. "What's going on here?" she demanded.

"I've got a few problems," Goodness said.

"You do?" Shirley muttered. "Well, you aren't the only one. My assignment's not working out the way it's supposed to."

Mercy frowned, and her gaze swung back to Goodness and then to Shirley again. "Do either of you have the feeling we might've been set up?"

Goodness sent her a puzzled glance. "What do you mean?"

"Think about it," Mercy said. "Shirley gets what would usually be a dream assignment. Just how hard can it be to give a boy a dog?"

"Well, actually, this prayer request is one of the most difficult ones I've ever received." She sighed. "Not only do we have the issue with Carter's father, there's this one dog that refuses to go away."

"I see."

"But under normal conditions, it wouldn't be difficult, would it?"

Shirley lifted one shoulder in a halfhearted shrug. "Not really. The thing that troubles me most is this dog. He doesn't seem...ordinary. And he simply won't leave. I think that problem's finally been solved, though. He's at the animal shelter and he'll probably be adopted soon."

"Good."

Shirley wore a sad frown. "Well, there's nothing I can do right now, so I've put the matter out of my mind. I'm here to help you two."

Mercy looked crestfallen. "My assignment's also failing."

"You don't happen to need a SWAT team, do you?" Goodness asked excitedly. It seemed a shame not to call out the big guns when they might be able to help her friends, too.

Mercy's expression was horrified. "Goodness, what are you thinking?"

She held up her hands. "Imagine this: helicopters descending, ropes dropping to the ground and men— young, handsome men—sliding down to the rooftops."

"To do what?" Mercy cried. "You'll ruin everything. I've got enough troubles with Harry and Rosalie as it is. I don't need *that* kind of help. Just the sound of those helicopters would send him into cardiac arrest."

"So what *can* we do?" Goodness asked. "We've got three unfinished assignments on our hands."

"At this point," Mercy suggested, "maybe we should let these situations play out and see what happens."

It seemed so little. But perhaps Mercy and Shirley were right. She'd done her best to bring Peter and Beth together, and her efforts, such as they were, had resulted in shock and confusion. Perhaps she should step aside and see what these humans could figure out for themselves.

Still, she *was* disappointed.

17

Carter had been weepy and sad ever since his father had driven him to the animal shelter where they'd left Rusty. All night long, he'd lain awake, thinking about his dog. He knew how bad his parents felt, so Carter tried not to show how miserable he was.

He realized his parents didn't have any extra money, and even the allowance he'd saved up wasn't enough.

"Carter," his mother called from the living room. "Come and see what your father brought home."

Hoping against hope that it was Rusty, Carter ran into the room. It wasn't. Instead, his mother stood in front of an artificial Christmas tree. The tree they had was dinky. So small, in fact, that it sat on the coffee table. It was in a flower pot and it was decorated with tiny glass balls. This one was real. Well, not exactly real because he could tell that the branches weren't like those of a live tree and it didn't have that nice Christmas smell. But it was real in size. And it came complete with strings of lights.

"A Christmas tree," his sister squealed with delight as she joined him in the living room. "Where did you get it?"

"Your father found it," his mother said. "On his way to work this morning, he caught a glimpse of something in an alley. He stopped, and there was the tree. Someone must've gotten a new tree because this one was propped up against a Dumpster. So your father brought it home for us."

That explained why Carter had heard his father return to the house shortly after he'd left for work.

Bailey clapped her hands. Even Carter smiled. It

was an old Christmas tree, a little worn and raggedy, but a whole lot better than the miniature one they had now. *That* one was more like a plant than a tree.

His first thought was that he wanted to show it to Rusty, except he couldn't because Rusty wasn't with him anymore. It hurt to remember his dog, but Carter couldn't think about anything else. He hoped Rusty would go to a good home and that someone in his new family would love him as much as Carter did.

"Do the lights work?" Bailey asked.

"We'll have to see," his mother said. She got down on the floor, crawled behind the tree and plugged in the cord. The lights flickered for a moment and then went out.

"That's probably why it was in the garbage," Carter told his mother.

"It's just a pretend tree," Bailey whined.

"It's pathetic-looking," Carter muttered. "But... it's okay." He tried to pretend he was happy about the Christmas tree, and he was, only...only it was old and the lights didn't work and no one else wanted it. That made him think of Rusty again. No one else had wanted him, either, but Carter did, in the worst way.

"We can make it look pretty," Bailey said, rebounding from her disappointment. "I have some colored paper from school and I could make an angel for the top," she said excitedly.

"We could string popcorn and cranberries, too," their mother suggested.

Carter didn't say anything for a long time. "I know how to cut out snowflakes," he finally told her.

"Thank you, Carter." As if recognizing how much effort it had taken him to offer, his mother hugged him tightly.

Carter tried to squirm out of her embrace. He was too big to have his mother hug him, but at the same time he kind of liked it. He didn't want his friends to know about it, though.

"We'll have the tree decorated when your father gets home from work," his mother said.

"Okay." Carter was willing to do his share.

Soon the aroma of popping corn filled the house. Carter sat at the kitchen table and patiently pierced the kernels with one of his mother's big sewing needles. He strung twenty-five kernels, then added a cranberry. Bailey decided to string her own and followed his pattern.

"Make it your own way," he snapped at his sister. "You don't have to do everything like me, you know."

"Carter," his mother said. "She just wants her string to match yours."

"Why can't she do her own design?"

"Because you're her big brother and she looks up to you."

Carter wanted to be angry, but he wasn't. His sister had helped him with Rusty and had loved the stray, too.

"What do you think Rusty's doing right now?" he asked his mother. "Will he remember me?"

"Of course he will," his mother said. "Rusty will always remember the boy who brought him food and washed the mud off his fur."

"And played catch with him."

Carter thought he might cry, but instead he smiled. Thinking about all the things he'd done with Rusty seemed to ease the ache in his heart.

The phone rang and his mother answered it quickly. "Hi, honey."

That meant it was his father.

"We're decorating the tree," his mother continued.

His father must've said something else because his mother went quiet.

Then she said, "Of course. He's right here." Placing her hand over the mouthpiece, she turned to Carter. "Your dad said he'd like to talk to you."

"Okay." Scooting off the chair, Carter took the phone. "Hi, Dad."

"How's it going?"

Carter shrugged. "All right, I guess."

"What do you think of the Christmas tree I found?"

"The lights don't work," he murmured.

"I'll take a look at those when I get home."

It was unusual for his father to work on Sundays. But he must've been putting in overtime at the restaurant. Christmas was a busy season and his father said they could use the money, so he worked as many overtime hours as he could get.

Carter wished his father was home the way he was

almost every Sunday. Usually they watched football together. If he'd been able to keep Rusty, then his dog
would've joined them. Carter was sure Rusty would
enjoy football as much as he did.

"You still feel bad about Rusty?"

"Yeah."

"So do I," his father admitted.

"I know."

"He's going to a good family and they'll love
Rusty, too."

But Carter didn't want any other family to love
Rusty. He wanted Rusty to be *his*. He hung his head.
"When will you be home?" he asked, his voice cracking.

"I'll get there as soon as I can."

"Bye, Dad."

"Bye, son."

Carter handed the phone back to his mother; before she hung up, their father spoke to Bailey, too.

Then he heard it.

A dog barking.

It sounded as if Rusty was right outside the door.
That wasn't possible, but it sure *sounded* like his dog.

"What's that noise?" his mother asked, frowning in his direction. She walked to the back door and opened it.

As Carter held his breath, he heard his mother cry out.

"Rusty!" Bailey shrieked.

"Rusty." Carter flew out of his chair so fast it went crashing backward onto the kitchen floor.

His mother opened the screen door and Rusty ran in, leaping up on his hind legs and dashing around in a circle and then jumping straight up in the air.

A moment later Rusty was licking Carter's face, yelping with joy. He flopped down on his belly, right in front of Carter, tail waving madly.

When Carter looked up at his mother, he saw that she had tears in her eyes. Soon she was down on the floor with him, hugging Rusty, too, along with Bailey. Even his sister was crying.

"How did he ever get here?" His mother stared at Carter.

He didn't have an answer for her. All he knew was that the animal shelter wasn't close by. It was miles and miles away.

Carter got a dish and filled it with water. Rusty lapped that up and ate every bit of popcorn on the floor.

"I'm not sure if popcorn's good for him or not," his mother warned.

Carter went to the cupboard for the cereal he'd fed him the day before. He prepared another large bowlful, with plenty of milk. His dog certainly wasn't a picky eater.

"Oh, Carter." His mother sighed deeply. "I don't know what your father's going to say about this."

"Don't call him at work," Carter pleaded. He was afraid his father would come home and take Rusty back to the shelter that very minute. He didn't want that to happen. Not yet. Not ever. Still, he realized his father wouldn't let Rusty stay, and he wanted to keep his dog with him as long as he could.

They finished stringing the popcorn and draping the strands on the tree. When Carter crawled underneath, Rusty came with him. With the dog at his side, Carter plugged the electrical cord in the socket again. This time the lights went on—and stayed on.

"Cool," his sister cried and clapped her hands.

"It's magic," Carter said. "Rusty brought it with him."

When they crawled out from under the tree, Rusty lay down on the carpet and rested his head on his paws. He looked about as tired as Carter felt, and he wondered if Rusty had stayed awake all night, thinking about Carter, the way Carter had about him. Unable to stop himself, Carter yawned.

"Why don't we all lie down for a bit," his mother suggested, eyeing him. It was almost as if she knew he'd hardly slept the night before.

"I don't take naps," Carter said indignantly. Bailey sometimes did. When she got cranky, their mother would send her into their bedroom. Bailey always fell asleep.

"It looks like Rusty's tired," his mother suggested. "I just thought you might want to keep him company."

"Oh."

Rusty followed Carter into his bedroom and lay on the rug beside his bed. Instead of climbing onto the mattress, Carter got down on the floor next to his dog. He flung his arm over Rusty and drifted off.

The next thing Carter heard was the sound of his father's voice.

"How is this possible?" his father was asking.

"Dad!" Carter leaped to his feet and tore into the kitchen, Rusty at his heels. "Did you hear?"

"Yes," his father said. "What I don't understand is how he found the house."

"But he did."

Rusty approached his father and gazed up at him.

His father bent down to pet Rusty's thick fur. "Well, my son said you were a special dog."

"Not only that," Carter rushed to tell his father, "when we first plugged in the tree, the lights only flickered and then they went out."

"And after Rusty got here, Carter plugged in the lights and they worked," Bailey said, so happy and excited that her words ran together.

Carter frowned at his sister. "*I* wanted to tell Dad that."

"Can he stay?" Ignoring him, Bailey turned to her father, eyes wide.

"I'm sorry, kids, we've already been through this."

"David, here's the number for the shelter," his mother said as she came into the room.

"I'm going to call and find out what happened." His father took the slip of paper and reached for the telephone. Carter stood by his side. He wanted to learn what had happened, too.

His father seemed to wait for a long time. Carter could hear the phone ringing. Holding the receiver away from his mouth, his dad muttered, "The shelter must be closed for the night."

Hope flared to life inside Carter. Maybe they'd have to keep Rusty overnight. Maybe—

"Hello," his father said, dashing Carter's hopes. "Yes, I understand the shelter's closed." He seemed to be listening. "We're the family who brought Rusty. He's the reddish stray that showed up in the schoolyard and followed my son home. I dropped Rusty off at the shelter yesterday afternoon. Well, Rusty's now here."

This announcement was followed by a short silence. Carter's father was shaking his head, as if the person on the other end of the line was arguing with him.

"I assure you he's here."

Another silence.

"Well, you might want to go and check his cage."

The person from the shelter must've said something else, because his father grew quiet once more. "He's going to check the cage where Rusty was put earlier," he told Carter.

The shelter employee was obviously back on the phone.

"Yes, he's here," his father explained for the third time. "I don't have a clue how he escaped or how he managed to get back to this house, but somehow or other, he did."

"Can he stay the night?" Carter pleaded. "Just one more night. Please, Dad, please."

"Yes, I'll bring him back in the morning," his father was saying.

Carter wrapped his arms around Rusty's neck. He had no idea how the dog had found his way across miles and miles of snow-covered roads to their house—but he'd always known Rusty possessed special powers.

His father hung up the phone. "He can only stay until morning, Carter."

Carter nodded. It wasn't long enough, but for this one last night, Rusty was his.

18

"They're here!" Rosalie shouted from the living room. Her voice rose with excitement. She'd gone to look out the window every few minutes, waiting for their daughter and her husband.

"Is it Donna?" Harry asked. He was no less excited than his wife.

"Yes," Rosalie said, letting the curtain fall back into place.

Harry struggled to get to his feet, and instantly Rosalie was at his side. She brought him the walker he hated and then slid her arm around his waist, guiding him into the hall.

"How do I look?" she asked.

Harry pretended to study her, noting her carefully combed hair, a soft lovely gray, and the antique cameo she wore with her dark green dress. "You couldn't be more beautiful if you'd tried."

"Oh, Harry."

At his words, Harry could see the blush of pleasure that crept across her cheeks.

The door opened and in breezed his daughter, with Richard, their son-in-law, both of them laden with parcels and bags. Soon everyone was kissing and hugging. Rosalie had tears in her eyes and, for that matter, so did Harry. Seeing his daughter renewed his waning strength.

All their married life, Rosalie had been a gracious hostess, and as soon as Donna and Richard had taken their coats off, she led them to the formal living room and brought out a tray of coffee and cookies.

Donna helped serve, and before long they were all

sitting together, chatting and catching up. Harry watched his daughter's animated gestures, and his heart swelled with love. In appearance, Donna resembled Rosalie's family, with her dark brown hair and eyes. Her personality, though, was all his. She was practical but enjoyed taking a risk now and then.

Donna was a teacher and had taught kindergarten and first grade for nearly thirty years. She was close to retirement, as was Richard. They'd met in college and married soon after. They'd presented him with two wonderful grandsons, two years apart.

"Tell me about Scotty," Rosalie said, eager for news of their youngest grandson. In a recent conversation, Donna had hinted that she had something special to share.

Donna and Richard smiled at each other, and Richard reached for his wife's hand.

"Scott's engaged!" Donna said happily.

"Is it Lana?" Harry asked. Their grandson had stopped by to visit in September and had brought a young woman to meet them. Harry recognized the look in his eyes. The boy was in love.

"Yes. Everyone likes Lana," Donna said. "We're all so pleased. Rich and I recently met her parents, and they're just as thrilled as we are."

"When's the wedding?" Rosalie asked.

"February," Donna told her mother.

"So soon!" his wife trilled, her eyes glowing. "Oh, I'm so glad."

"Lana wanted to wait for June," Donna said, "but Scott said a Valentine wedding was more romantic."

"Who would've guessed that about Scott?" Richard asked.

Rosalie glanced at Harry and they exchanged a smile. "He gets his romantic heart from his grandfather."

"Dad?" Donna did an exaggerated double take.

"Your father's sent me flowers every Valentine's Day since the year we met. Even during the war." Her eyes filled with tears as she looked at him. Pulling her lace-edged handkerchief from her sleeve, she dabbed her cheeks. "This is such good news, isn't it, dear?"

Harry nodded. All his grandchildren would be married now. Although Harry had only met Lana that one time, he believed the young woman was a good match for his youngest grandson.

"That's not our only news," Donna said. Once again she smiled at Richard. "Phillip called last week and Tiffany's pregnant."

Rosalie squealed with delight.

"Rich and I are going to be grandparents."

"Oh, my goodness," Rosalie said, clasping her hands. "That means Harry and I will be *great*-grandparents."

"You're much too young to be a great-grandmother," Harry teased, just so he could watch Rosalie blush once more.

"Nonsense," his wife countered. "Some of our friends are great-grandparents several times over."

That was true, and Harry didn't bother to comment. He'd hoped to live long enough to meet his first great-grandchild but that wasn't to be.

Richard helped himself to another cookie. Rosalie had picked them up at the bakery on Saturday, and although he wouldn't tell her this, Harry thought they were as good as any she might have baked. Actually, he wouldn't mind a second one himself. As soon as he stretched out his arm, Rosalie immediately lifted the platter and offered it to him.

Donna was still talking about the baby. She'd be the perfect grandmother, Harry knew. She'd been an excellent mother, and after all those years spent teaching six- and seven-year-olds, she had a real way with kids. Donna's students loved her; it wasn't unusual for teenagers and adults to come and see her—people, who at one time, had been in her class.

"When's Tiffany due?" Rosalie asked.

"July," Donna said. "We don't know if it's a boy or a girl, although I don't think anyone really cares. The timing is certainly good."

Richard smiled. "Phillip's out of graduate school now and the job he got with Microsoft seems secure. Or as secure as any corporate job is these days." He turned to Harry, who nodded. Over the years, they'd often discussed the economy and related issues.

"Phillip does a bit more traveling than either of them would like," Donna added, "but he's in training, so that goes with the territory."

Richard sipped his coffee. "I understand the two of you are planning to sell the house," he said.

Rosalie sighed and aimed a sad smile at Harry.

"Unfortunately we had some bad news regarding Liberty Orchard," Harry told him. In retrospect he'd give just about anything to have handed the administrator a check for the deposit the day they'd toured the facility. "Apparently the only available unit has already been taken."

Donna leaned forward. "That's what Mom said, so I phoned Liberty Orchard and talked to Elizabeth Goldsmith myself."

"She can't wave a magic wand and make another unit appear." Harry didn't want to admit how much the news depressed him. This was to be his last gift to Rosalie before he died, and now it wasn't going to happen.

"When I phoned," Donna went on to say, "Ms. Goldsmith said she was just about to contact you."

"The unit's available?" Harry felt a surge of hope.

"Not the one you originally saw, but another one."

"Did someone die?" Rosalie asked, frowning.

"No, it belonged to a couple. Perhaps you met them. Ralph and Daisy—I can't remember their last name."

"McDonald," Harry supplied. He remembered talking with the two and had quite liked them. Their children both lived in Chicago. "Are they moving closer to their son and daughter?"

"Yes."

"When?" Rosalie asked.

"They hope to be out by the fifth of January. It'll take a couple of days to give the unit a thorough cleaning and then it'll be ready for you and Dad by the tenth."

"I'll get them a check right after Christmas," Harry said, unable to hide his pleasure.

"It's all taken care of, Dad," Donna said. "I knew you'd want the unit, so Rich and I put it on our credit card."

"I'll get the check to you then. Immediately." The fact that they'd used credit bothered him; he couldn't help it.

Donna gestured magnanimously. "Consider it your Christmas gift."

Harry wouldn't allow his daughter to do that; still, the certainty of acquiring the unit afforded him real peace of mind.

"That's wonderful news," Rosalie agreed, nodding vigorously.

"It's even better than you realize," Donna said. "I'll be here the entire time to help you move."

"What about school?" Harry asked.

Donna smiled. "That's my other surprise. I'm retiring. As of now."

Harry stared at her. "But…it's the middle of the school year."

"Actually, this is a good news/bad news situation," Rich explained. "Donna needs knee-replacement surgery."

Their daughter nodded. "I guess that's what I get from all those years of crawling around on the floor with my kindergarten classes. It isn't extensive surgery, but it'll require several weeks of rehab. I'd already decided to retire at the end of this school year. But with the wedding, the surgery and the baby, Rich and I felt it made more sense to do it now."

"I think this is wonderful," Rosalie said again.

Rosalie had always supported their children's decisions, even when they gave Harry pause. She was loyal to a fault; he loved that about her.

"The paperwork's been turned in and everything's a go."

"You should've told us," Rosalie chastised.

"I couldn't until I got the final word. I didn't mean to hide it from you, Mom, but I know how you worry."

While Donna claimed it was the surgery, the wedding and the baby, Harry suspected there was another reason his daughter had chosen to retire early. "So you'll help us pack up the house," he said.

"Absolutely. Lorraine, too."

This was welcome news to Harry. His prayer had been answered—they had a place at Liberty Orchard now. And his daughters would both be here. If God should choose to bring him home, Harry could be assured that Rosalie would be well looked after.

This was going to be the best Christmas of his life. And the last…

19

Beth yawned. It'd been a long day, beginning with church that morning and then brunch with her family. Now, at almost ten, she was tired and ready for bed. She'd logged on to World of Warcraft a little while ago and was disappointed to discover that Peter wasn't online. Still, she felt relieved that they'd decided to postpone their meeting until after New Year's. That gave her time to make a few decisions, time to assess the situation and consider how to deal with what she'd learned.

The doorbell chimed. Beth frowned, wondering who'd stop by this late at night.

When she checked the peephole, she saw a lovely woman standing in the hallway. Whoever it was had the most incredible blue eyes. Beth didn't recognize her. But even though she didn't know who this woman was, she unlatched the door and opened it.

Instead of the woman she'd seen through the peephole, a man stood there in front of her. Not just any man. John Nicodemus, her ex-husband.

Peter.

If Beth was shocked, it was nothing compared to the look on Peter's face.

"*Marybeth?*" he whispered as if he couldn't seem to find his voice. "What are you doing here?"

"I live here."

"No, you don't," he argued.

"Are you looking for Borincana?" she asked.

Peter went pale.

"You're Timixie," she added. It was obvious that they both needed to sit down, so she stepped out of the doorway and waved him inside.

Peter moved into the living room and sank heavily onto the sofa. Elbows balanced on his knees, he thrust his fingers through his hair and stared down at the floor.

Beth understood exactly how he felt because she'd experienced the very same mix of emotions when she'd seen him in Leavenworth. It had felt as if the sidewalk had started to crumble beneath her feet. The shock had been followed by anger and disbelief.

Yesterday in Leavenworth, she'd suspected him of somehow arranging this. As she watched his face, she could see that he was feeling doubt, incredulity, suspicion—just as she had.

"How can this be?" he murmured after several minutes.

"I asked myself that, too."

His eyes narrowed. "How long have you known?"

She wanted it understood that she hadn't arranged this, any more than he had. "Since Leavenworth."

His mouth tightened. "You were there?"

Beth nodded. "You were standing by the gazebo, exactly as we'd agreed. Then I saw that red rose and I nearly fainted."

"Who was on the phone?" he demanded. "I would've recognized your voice."

"My friend Heidi. She's a new friend—you never met her."

He straightened, then leaned back against the sofa as he absorbed her words.

"Why are you here?" she asked. Beth studied him carefully. He was even more attractive than she remembered. The years had matured him, and his features had lost their boyish quality. He looked more serious now, more...adult. They'd both been so juvenile and irrational, so quick to get out of the relationship. Beth had felt blindsided by the pain of it and she thought that John...Peter might have been, too. Certainly, his online confidences suggested as much.

"I shouldn't have come," he muttered. "The whole time I was driving here, I couldn't figure out why I was doing this."

Beth didn't understand it, either. They'd already said they'd wait until after New Year's.

He closed his eyes for a few seconds, then opened them again and looked directly at her. "This afternoon we made our plans but all of a sudden that wasn't good enough. I couldn't stop thinking about you. I was afraid that if we delayed meeting again, neither of us would ever be ready. It was just too easy to keep putting it off."

Beth could see that was true.

"Once I made the decision, waiting even an hour seemed intolerable. I had your address from the phone call in Leavenworth—thanks to your friend, as it turns out. I decided to meet you and I didn't care that it was after nine at night and I was coming uninvited."

"Only you *had* met me."

"Well, I could hardly know that, could I?" he snapped, then seemed to regret his outburst. "How did something like this happen?" he asked helplessly.

She responded with a question of her own. "When did John become Peter?"

"When I began working in the corporate office at Starbucks. There were four Johns, so I decided to use my middle name and I just got used to it. The only people who call me John these days are my parents."

In other words, his name change had come about

in a perfectly rational way—it was certainly no attempt at subterfuge.

"What about you, Mary*beth?*"

"Marybeth became Beth after the divorce."

He regarded her skeptically. "Any particular reason?"

"I wanted a new start, and Marybeth sounded so
childish and outdated to me, so I shortened it to Beth.
The only people who still call me Marybeth are my
family."

"I see." He rubbed his face. "I don't mean to be forward here, but I could use a cup of coffee."

"Of course. I'm sorry, I should've asked." She stood
and took two steps toward the kitchen before abruptly
turning back. "How'd you do that, by the way?"

"Do what?"

"I checked the peephole in my door before I un-
locked it and there was a woman on the other side."

"A woman?" He wore a puzzled frown.

"She was attractive and had blond hair and striking
blue eyes."

"It wasn't me."

"Obviously."

He met her gaze head-on. "I was the only one there, Beth. Maybe you should have your eyesight examined."

"Maybe you should—" She clamped her mouth shut. They had too many other things to discuss. An argument would be pointless; it didn't matter what or whom she'd seen—or *thought* she'd seen. "Give me a minute to make that coffee."

Unexpectedly, Peter followed her into the kitchen. "What just happened back there?" he asked with obvious surprise.

"What do you mean?" She efficiently measured the grounds and poured water into the coffeemaker.

"You dropped the discussion."

Confused, Beth glanced over at him. "What discussion?"

"It used to be that you absolutely *had* to be right," he told her. "You'd go ten miles out of your way to prove how right you were and how wrong I was."

"I did?" Beth didn't remember it like that.

"You always had a point to prove."

"Yes, well, people change."

Peter didn't speak for some time. "I've changed, too."

"I'm sure we both have." For the better, although she didn't say that. After six months of being his partner on WoW, she knew this man, knew important things about his character, and he wasn't like her ex-husband at all.

The coffee started to drip and Beth got two mugs from the cupboard. Staring down at the kitchen counter, she gathered her courage to ask him a question.

"Did you mean what you said this afternoon about…still loving me?" The words seemed to stick in her throat.

"Yes."

She wished he'd elaborate—and a moment later he did.

"I never stopped loving you, Marybeth. That was one of the problems. For years, the people closest to me have encouraged me to find someone else and remarry. I tried."

She jerked up her head. "So it's true?" Abruptly her

heart sank, and she actually felt ill. "You did marry again."

"No," he returned vehemently. "Who told you that?"

"A friend. Well, sort of a friend. Lisa Carroll. Remember her?"

"Yeah." Peter frowned. "She told you that?" When Beth nodded, he pressed his palms on the kitchen counter. "That isn't even *close* to being true. Why would she do that?" He paused. "What about you? Have you...did you find someone else?"

Beth shrugged, unwilling to disclose that she'd been practically a hermit in the dating world. "I went out some. No one for long."

"I occasionally dated, too," he confessed. "Including Lisa," he added in a low voice. "For about two weeks."

Well, that explains it, Beth thought—but didn't say.

"No one clicked with me," she said after a brief silence.

He offered her a sad smile. "No one clicked with me, either."

"Mostly I was afraid." Because she needed something to do with her hands, she filled the two mugs with coffee, welcoming the distraction.

Peter reached for his mug and she automatically opened her refrigerator and took out the milk.

He smiled. "You remember that I take milk in my coffee."

"How could I forget?" she asked, a smile tugging at the corners of her own mouth. "Don't you remember we had that huge fight over milk? I'd forgotten to pick some up on my way home."

Peter threw back his head and stared at the ceiling. "I was pretty unreasonable back then."

She'd thought the same thing. He'd accused her of intentionally forgetting the milk, apparently convinced that she'd done it in retaliation, since he'd been right in a silly argument they'd had the day before. It'd all been so stupid, so adolescent.

Peter poured a dollop of milk into his coffee, then returned the carton to the refrigerator. Beth watched in amazement. While they were married, he'd driven her to the brink of insanity by leaving everything out. He left drawers open, newspapers on the floor, dirty dishes everywhere.

When she complained, he'd accused her of being

too fastidious and a "neat freak." Beth hadn't seen herself as either; however she'd considered him lazy and disorganized—and had told him so.

They both sipped their coffee for a couple of minutes, leaning casually against the kitchen counters. Despite her relaxed pose, Beth felt anything but.

"Did you mean what *you* said?" Peter gazed at her over the top of his mug.

She knew what he was asking. "I always loved you. Even when I filed for divorce, I loved you. I couldn't live with you, but that didn't change how I felt about you."

He chuckled softly and nodded. "It was the same with me. You were driving me crazy."

"We did it to each other." Beth set her mug on the counter. "So," she said, sighing. "This afternoon you said you don't want to look back and that it's time to move forward."

He nodded again. "It's time for *both* of us to let go of the past, Marybeth."

"And...what about the future?"

He didn't answer right away. He glanced at her, his

eyes uncertain, then looked away. "In other words, you're asking where we go from here."

"It's a fair question, don't you think?"

"I agree. Only I'm not sure what to say. Is it just a coincidence that we've been online together for the past six months and neither of us realized it?"

"I never dreamed it could be you," she said. "I didn't set this up... I wouldn't know how."

"I believe you. I couldn't have, either."

Suddenly she recalled the conversation she'd had with her mother and the fact that Joyce had even lit a candle in church on her behalf. She took a deep breath. "It seems to me that we were brought back together for a reason."

"Yes."

Beth's heart pounded frantically as Peter put down his mug and walked around the counter to stand in front of her. He settled his hands on her shoulders and stared into her eyes.

"If you're willing to give us another chance, I think we should do it," he said in an urgent voice.

Beth gave him a tentative smile. "I'm willing."

That was when he kissed her. As he lowered his mouth to hers, Beth closed her eyes and slipped her arms around him. His lips were soft, pliable, warm. The years fell away, and it was as if they were college students again, hungry for each other, desperately in love and ready to take on dragons and warriors and despots and worse.

Beth eased her mouth from his. "Do you want to spend Christmas with me and my family?" she asked, smiling up at him.

Peter laughed. "If you'll spend New Year's with mine."

"Very clever, Goodness," Mercy said, sitting on the counter in Beth Fischer's kitchen, swinging her feet.

"I had to do something," Goodness told her. "Peter and Beth were content to delay their meeting, so I had to put an end to *that*." She turned to Mercy and smiled. "I've learned men are much more suggestible than women."

"I've discovered the same thing," Shirley said, joining them. "That wasn't all, though. Stepping in front of Peter when he arrived at Beth's so she saw your face instead of his was brilliant."

"Tricky, too." Mercy's voice was admiring. Goodness had to reveal herself to Beth, yet remain hidden from Peter. Not an easy task and if Gabriel ever found out, she'd never hear the end of it.

"Gabriel will be pleased when he learns Beth and Peter are together again."

"I think he will, too," Goodness said.

Her mission had been completed.

The candle Joyce Fischer had lit in the church flickered one last time and then went out.

20

That night, knowing Rusty would have to go back to the animal shelter, Carter settled the dog on his bed. Placing both arms around him, Carter spoke softly in his ear.

"You're the best dog any kid could have," he whispered.

As if he understood the words, Rusty licked Carter's face. He seemed to be saying that Carter was the best friend he'd ever have, too.

"I'd do anything to keep you. Well…almost anything." After his father had come home from work and explained that they'd be taking Rusty back to the shelter in the morning, Carter had seriously considered running away.

If his mom and dad weren't going to let him have Rusty, then Carter decided he no longer wanted to be part of this family. He'd find another family, one that could afford a dog and kept promises.

He had over thirty dollars saved from his allowance, which should be enough to get him to his grandparents' house in Wenatchee. He was sure that if they knew about Rusty, Grandma and Grandpa Parker would pay whatever it cost to keep him.

But in the end, Carter couldn't do it. He couldn't run away. He loved his mother and father and even his little sister, although she was a pest most of the time.

"I'll go back to the shelter with you," Carter assured his friend. In the morning he'd ride down with his father. He was determined to speak to the lady who'd taken Rusty before.

Carter wanted to make *sure* his dog went to a good home. Not just a regular home, either. The very best.

Carter had prayed for a dog and he'd prayed hard. Although he loved Rusty, maybe—despite everything—this wasn't the dog God meant for him.

Tears welled up in his eyes and he tried to hold back a sniffle. He didn't want his sister to hear him crying, so he buried his face in the dog's fur.

"I want to keep Rusty, too," Bailey whispered from the other side of the room.

Carter pretended not to hear.

"I love Rusty just as much as you do," she said, only louder this time.

"I know."

She sniffled once and then Carter did, too. "Go to sleep," he said.

Bailey didn't answer, and Carter suspected she felt as sad as he did. Even if Rusty belonged to him, he was willing to share his dog with Bailey. Not every day; just some of the time—once a week or so.

Except that Rusty wouldn't be his to share. His

friend would be with him for only a few more hours. The realization was crushing.

"Go to sleep," he repeated and hugged Rusty closer.

"This is a fine mess you've gotten yourself into," Mercy muttered, glaring at Shirley. They were both inside the children's bedroom. Shirley sat on the foot of the bed, where Rusty lay tightly curled up next to Carter's feet.

"Me?" Shirley wore a look of innocence as she continued to pet the dog.

"Yes, you." Mercy pointed an accusing finger at her fellow Prayer Ambassador. Then she crossed her arms as she surveyed the sleeping children, lost in their dreams.

"How could you have let this happen?" Mercy asked.

Shirley straightened defensively.

Mercy wasn't fooled. "*You're* the one who stopped by the animal shelter and conveniently opened the cage and set Rusty free."

"Ah…"

"That wasn't the only door you opened, either." Mercy was on to her friend's antics and she wasn't going to let Shirley squirm out of this one.

"Well…" Shirley shifted uncomfortably. As though aware of their presence, Rusty lifted his head and looked around.

"It's all right, boy," Shirley whispered, reassuring the dog.

Rusty put his head down on his paws and closed his eyes once more.

"Don't bother to deny that you're the one who set him free," Mercy said in a stern voice.

"All right," Shirley confessed. "That was me—"

"I thought so."

"I couldn't help it! Carter loves that dog, and Rusty loves him. The two of them are *meant* to be together."

"Not according to what you first said." Although she made it sound like a complaint, Mercy was actually delighted with her friend. In the past, Shirley had been a real stickler for protocol during their earthly visitations. The former guardian angel always took on the role of supervisor, policing Goodness and Mercy as if that was her right. She found it gratifying that, for once, Shirley had broken the rules herself.

"Just look at Carter and Rusty," Shirley urged. "How can anyone take that dog away from that little boy?"

Mercy gazed down at the sleeping figures. Rusty slept peacefully close to Carter and Mercy was moved almost to tears by their mutual devotion.

"What's going to happen now?" Mercy asked.

"I don't know." Shirley shook her head. "I pleaded Carter's case to Gabriel. That's all I can do."

"You did?" Many a time Mercy had done the same, but to no avail. She didn't think Shirley had gone to the archangel even once to request assistance. Until now.

"What did he say?"

Shirley cleared her throat. "He said I'd already interfered where I shouldn't have. That God has everything under control."

"So he knew what you'd done." This shouldn't surprise Mercy. Gabriel always seemed to be aware of their every move.

"I'm to butt out." She sounded a little affronted, and Mercy couldn't blame her.

"Gabriel told you that?"

"In exactly those words, too. He warned me that I'm not to involve myself in any way from this point forward. He did ask me to stick around, though."

"I should hope so."

Shirley glanced down at the floor. "Gabriel wasn't happy with me."

Mercy shrugged, as if to imply that should be expected. "Don't worry about it. Gabriel knew what he was doing when he sent us back to earth."

Shirley nodded morosely.

Seeing that her friend felt bad, Mercy decided to inject a bit of entertainment into their visit to Leavenworth. "Want to have some fun?"

As little as a week ago, Shirley would have sharply chastised Mercy for even suggesting such a thing. This time she simply gazed at her. "What do you have in mind?"

"Have you noticed the ornaments hanging from the streetlamps?" Actually, they were pretty hard to miss. The town council had hung large wreaths, candy canes and candles, interspersed with a few unrealistic-looking angels.

"I was thinking," Mercy went on, "of rearranging the ornaments, mixing things up a bit."

"We could make all the ornaments that aren't angels disappear," Shirley said tentatively, entering into the spirit of the enterprise.

"I like it," Mercy said excitedly.

"Let's contact Goodness and get started."

Tonight was December twenty-third, and they had one last day on earth. Christmas Eve, they'd have to return to heaven for the celebration. Only one day left, and Mercy intended to make the most of it.

Carter was tucked warmly in his bed when Rusty began to bark. The barking became louder and more frantic and it didn't stop. At first Carter ignored it, trying to sleep. But when he finally forced open his eyes, he couldn't see. The entire bedroom was filled with fog. There was a horrible smell. Like something burning.

The fog was so thick he couldn't even see his sister's bed. He choked. Taking a breath was painful.

Completely disoriented, he sat up.

"Bailey?"

His sister didn't answer.

"Bailey!" He tried again.

All at once, the bedroom door burst open and was shut with a bang. Out of the fog, his father emerged with his hand cupped over his nose and mouth.

"Dad? What's happening?"

"Fire," his father said tersely. It wasn't fog then, but smoke. Carter's dad swooped him off the bed and into his arms. He stumbled across the room, carrying Carter, then set him down and reached for Bailey. Jerking open the bedroom window, he gently dropped her, bare feet and all, into the snow.

"Get away from the house as fast as you can," he said. "Your mother's out front waiting for you."

Carter watched his sister race through the snow.

The smoke that was now pouring out of the bedroom window made Carter's eyes smart. He was next. His father lowered him carefully into the snow, then looked over his shoulder and leaped out himself.

Father and son ran hand in hand around the side of the house.

In the distance, Carter heard the wail of a fire engine, the alarm piercing the night.

His house was on fire.

His mother cried out with relief when she saw Carter and his father. Sobbing, she held out her arms. She swept Carter into her embrace and started kissing him. He hugged her tight and felt the tears on her cheeks.

The fire truck arrived and suddenly there were all kinds of people in front of the house. The paramedic put Carter and his family inside the aid car and checked their vital signs. His father had to breathe into an oxygen mask for a few minutes.

When Carter looked out the back of the aid car, he saw flames shooting up through the roof. The firefighters had the hoses going, and there seemed to be a dozen men and women at work.

"What woke you up?" The question came from the man who'd given his father the mask.

Carter answered. "Rusty." All of a sudden he realized he didn't know where his dog was. Bolting to his feet, Carter screamed, "Where's Rusty?" even though it hurt his throat to do that.

His father removed the mask. "My son's dog was barking," he said hoarsely. "If it hadn't been for Rusty, I would never have been able to get my family out of that house."

"Where's Rusty? Where's Rusty?" Carter cried, looking frantically in all directions. The thought of his dog still inside terrified him.

Then the sound of Rusty's bark cut through the night.

"Rusty!" Carter jumped out of the aid car as the dog raced across the neighbor's yard toward him. Getting down on one knee in the snow, Carter wrapped his arms around the dog's neck and hugged him. "You saved us. You saved us," he whispered again and again.

His father joined Carter and knelt down next to him and the dog.

"Well, boy," David said and his voice was shaking. "We still can't afford a dog, but you've earned your way into our home for the rest of your life."

"Do you mean it, Dad?"

"Every word."

"Rusty," Carter choked out. Rusty *was* his dog, just

the way he'd always hoped, just the way he wanted. Tears fell from his eyes and Rusty repeatedly licked his face.

"All I can say," the man inside the aid car told them, "is that you're mighty lucky you had that dog."

"It wasn't luck," Carter insisted. "Rusty's the dog God sent me."

The medic nodded. "You've got all the proof you need of that."

21

Lorraine and her husband, Kenny, had arrived early on Christmas Eve. Now it was two o'clock, and Rosalie was busy in the kitchen with her daughters, getting everything ready for dinner that evening. Richard and Ken sat with Harry in the family room, watching a football game on television. Two of the grandchildren would come later that afternoon.

This was all the Christmas Harry needed. With his children and two of his four grandchildren close, he was at peace.

Rising from his chair was difficult, and embarrassed by his need for it, Harry groped for the walker.

"You need any help with that, Dad?" Richard asked.

"No, I'm fine. A little slow, but fine." A bit wobbly on his feet, he glanced over at the two men who'd married his daughters. He loved them as much as he did Lorraine and Donna. They were the sons he'd never had. It was through their children that Harry and Rosalie would live on.

"Where are you going, Dad?" Lorraine asked, stepping out of the kitchen, wiping her hands on a dish towel. Harry didn't know what they were cooking in there, but it sure smelled good.

"I thought I'd rest for a while before dinner."

She put her arm around his waist and walked him down the hallway to the master bedroom.

Inside the room, Harry sat on the edge of his bed and Lorraine placed the walker where he could reach it once he awoke.

"I'm grateful to have this moment alone with you," he said to his oldest daughter.

"What is it, Dad?" She sat on the bed beside him.

"After I'm gone, I'll need you to look after your mother. You and Donna."

"You know we will." Tears filled her eyes.

Harry took her hand and squeezed it. "I don't want there to be tears when I pass, understand?"

"Oh, Dad, of course there'll be tears. You have no idea how much you're loved. You're the very heart of our family."

Harry sighed, knowing their sadness couldn't be avoided. Death for him, though, would be freeing. "Donna will be here to help your mother with the move."

"Kenny and I plan to come, as well."

"Thank you." Harry wasn't sure he'd still be around by then. But everything had been set in motion, and that brought him a sense of peace. "I think I'd better rest for a while."

"Good idea." When he lay down on the quilt, she kissed him on the cheek, then rearranged his pillows.

He'd just closed his eyes when Rosalie came into the room. "How are you feeling, sweetheart?" she asked.

"I'm tired, that's all."

She picked up the afghan at the foot of the bed and

covered him gently. "Rest now, and I'll wake you in time for dinner."

Harry nodded, and then, as his wife of sixty-six years was about to leave the room, he reached for her hand.

Rosalie turned back expectantly.

"I've always loved you, my Rose."

She smiled softly. "I know, Harry. And you're the love of my life."

"This life and the next."

Rosalie bent down to kiss his cheek, and Harry closed his eyes.

"Harry," Mercy whispered.

Harry Alderwood's eyes flickered open and he stared at her in astonishment. "Am I dead? In heaven?"

Mercy nodded. "Look," she said, with a gesture that swept from his head to his feet. "You're not old anymore. You're young again."

"Rosalie?"

"You'll see her soon," Mercy promised him. "And when she gets here, she'll be the young woman you met all those years ago."

"I saw you before," Harry said, pointing at Mercy. "That night I forgot my walker."

Mercy smiled. "That was me."

"You helped me, and I'm most appreciative."

Shirley, Goodness and Mercy surrounded Harry. "Come with us," Mercy said. "Your parents and your brother are waiting for you."

"Mom and Dad?" he asked excitedly. "And Ted, too?"

Mercy smiled again. "Everyone. All of heaven has been waiting for your arrival. We're celebrating Christmas and you'll see—it's nothing like it is on earth."

Gabriel appeared before them. "Harry Alderwood?"

Harry, young and handsome, nodded.

"Welcome to Paradise," Gabriel said. "I'll take over from here." The archangel looked at the three Prayer Ambassadors, dismissing them. "I'll be joining you shortly."

Shirley, Goodness and Mercy stood in the choir loft at Leavenworth First Christian Church for the seven o'clock Christmas Eve service. Once they were finished here, they'd join Beth and her family at Midnight Mass in Seattle.

As the organ music swelled with the opening strains of "O Holy Night," Goodness leaned over to her friends. "Just wait until these humans hear the music in heaven. Boy, are they in for a surprise."

"Like Harry," Mercy said. She'd served God as a Prayer Ambassador but she'd never assisted in the crossing before now. Watching as the frail body of Harry Alderwood was transformed into that of a young man had been a moving experience. His spirit had been set free from his weak and failing heart, free from his pain and free from the restraints of the world.

"Like Harry," Gabriel agreed, suddenly standing beside them. He focused his attention on Mercy. "You did well."

"Thank you," she said humbly. "I'm glad I was there to escort him to heaven."

"How's his family doing?" Mercy asked, concerned for Rosalie and Harry's daughters. She couldn't imagine what it must've been like for Rosalie to come into the bedroom and find that her husband had died in his sleep.

"It's never easy for those on earth to lose a loved one," Gabriel told them.

"They don't understand, do they?"

"Not yet," Gabriel said. "For now, they're looking through a dim glass. Soon, each one will know, each one will have his or her own experience and understand that death is not just an end but a beginning. A true beginning."

"How's Rosalie?"

"At the moment, she's overwhelmed by grief. Her daughters are with her, though, and their love will sustain her. One or both of them will stay here until she's settled in Liberty Orchard."

That reassured Mercy.

The music came to a halt and the minister, Pastor Williams, stepped over to the podium in the front of the church.

"I have two announcements to make before we proceed with the Christmas program," he said. "I've received word that Harry Alderwood passed away this afternoon. I ask that we keep Rosalie and her family in our prayers."

Hushed murmurs rippled through the congregation.

"Also, as many of you know, the Jacksons lost their home in a fire last night. Fortunately, they have insurance. However, all their belongings have been destroyed. They're staying with relatives in Wenatchee right now, but if the people of our community could open their hearts to this young family, I know you will be blessed."

"That's Carter's family," Shirley said, glancing at her friends.

"Ah yes, Carter," Gabriel muttered, turning a suspicious look on Shirley.

"I promise you I didn't have anything to do with the house fire," she said, holding up her hands.

"I know—because the three of you were out rearranging the street displays."

"Ah…" Mercy stared down at her feet. It was just a little thing, something they'd done for enjoyment. Surely Gabriel wouldn't mind. The residents didn't seem to.

"You knew about the fire?" Shirley asked the archangel.

"I did."

"What happened?" Clearly, curiosity was getting the better of her. "How did it start?"

Gabriel leaned against the railing in the choir loft. "You remember that Christmas tree David Jackson found by the Dumpster?" he asked.

"Yes..."

"There was a reason it'd been thrown away."

"It shorted out?"

Gabriel nodded. "Carter's mother didn't turn off the lights when they went to bed because she was afraid that once she did, they wouldn't come back on." He sighed. "Foolishly they hadn't checked the batteries in their smoke alarm."

"Oh, dear."

"The fire, while devastating, will work out well for the family. The insurance will take care of replacing their earthly possessions. David, Carter's father, will soon be offered a new job at higher pay."

"And his mother?"

"She'll get that job with the school district and the family will be able to afford Rusty without a problem."

"That's wonderful news," Goodness said.

"What about Rusty?" Shirley asked.

"He'll live a good life and a long one. Rusty will be Carter's constant companion. They'll remain close until Rusty dies when he's sixteen human years old."

"Oh-h-h," all three of them breathed.

"Carter will remember his dog for the rest of his life." Gabriel touched Shirley's arm. "Well done."

Shirley beamed at his praise.

"Tell us about Beth Fischer," Goodness said.

"Ah, yes, Beth and Peter. They're going to step into church right now." In the blink of an eye, it was almost midnight. The three Prayer Ambassadors and Gabriel made the transition from Leavenworth First Christian to St. Alphonsus Catholic Church in Seattle.

The loft was crowded with members of the choir, resplendent in their long red robes. The music had just begun when Goodness saw Beth walking into the church with Peter at her side. A smile came over her as Beth and Peter entered the pew where the Fischer family was sitting.

Even from this distance, Goodness could see the

surprise on Joyce Fischer's face as Beth gestured toward Peter. Soon Joyce and Peter were hugging.

"What'll happen with them?" Goodness asked. "Do they remarry?"

Gabriel grinned. "Yes, they'll wed just a few weeks from now. They've both learned from their mistakes."

"They'll have children, won't they?"

"Three," Gabriel said. "Two boys and a girl."

"Please tell me they won't name their children after their characters from World of Warcraft." Goodness grimaced and shook her head.

Gabriel laughed. "Don't worry. The oldest boy will be John, the daughter Mary and the youngest boy's going to be named Tim."

"For Timixie?"

"You'll have to ask them."

"I can?" Goodness squealed excitedly.

"Not for many years but in time, yes, you'll have that opportunity."

Goodness couldn't possibly have looked more pleased.

"I believe we're late," Gabriel said, ushering the three toward heaven.

"Silent Night" played softly at the church as Gabriel, along with Shirley, Goodness and Mercy, returned to heaven, where the joyous celebration of the Savior's birth was about to take place.

"Peace on earth," Gabriel murmured as they ascended.

"And goodwill to all mankind," Shirley added. "Dogs, too."

Goodness and Mercy laughed as the gates of heaven opened to bring them home.